Bicentennial Eve:
A Wisconsin Novella

Reading Julie A. Jacob's *Bicentennial Eve* is like spending the day with close friends. From Grandma Kitty out for an adventure she's been waiting seventy years to tackle, to her new teen granddaughter Skylar looking for her first kiss, this poignant story of a family's day in 1976 and beyond will touch readers. Well done.

—**Lisa Lickel**, *Creative Wisconsin* magazine editor and author of the Forces of Nature series

Step into the heart of 1976 Wisconsin, where the spirit of America's bicentennial pulses through every page. In *Bicentennial Eve*, Julie A. Jacob delivers an evocative, unforgettable portrait of a family on the brink of change. A young girl aches for her first kiss, a college student is caught between adventure abroad and love at home, and a devoted husband is left wondering what his wife truly desires. Brimming with nostalgia, longing, and the quiet hope of new beginnings, this gentle novel invites you to relive the magic and heartbreak of a pivotal moment in history. Perfect for fans of rich family dramas and coming-of-age tales, *Bicentennial Eve* will leave you reflecting on the ties that bind and the dreams that set us free.

—**Marie Zhuikov**, author of *The Path of Totality*

Bicentennial Eve:
A Wisconsin Novella

by
Julie A. Jacob

Printed in the United States of America

Fresh Water Press, LLC
P.O. Box 425
Two Rivers, WI

Cover design by Vagabond Creative Studio
Author photo credit: Stephanie Bartz

ISBN Paperback: 979-8-9988953-1-9
ISBN Kindle: 979-8-9988953-2-6
ISBN eBook: 979-8-9988953-3-3

Library of Congress Control Number: 2026933928

DEDICATION

For Peter

JANSEN FAMILY TREE

Kitty Barrett
Born September 18, 1902

Frederick Jansen
Born August 21, 1900
Died November 14, 1960

Vivian Jansen
Born August 15, 1925

Michael Jansen
Born February 12, 1924
Died June 7, 1944

Claire Jansen
Born July 18, 1932
Married June 18, 1955

Joe Ames
Born February 2, 1930
Married June 18, 1955

Skylar Ames
Born June 22, 1963

Grace Ames
Born October 5, 1958

AMES FAMILY TREE

Chester Barrett
(Kitty's younger brother)
Born December 9, 1904
Married Edna June 17, 1958

Edna Kowalski
Born April 5, 1903
Married Harry July 27, 1929
Divorced November 3, 1947
Married Chester June 17, 1958

Harry Ames
Born March 2, 1900
Died November 8, 1950

Amy Lange
Born August 15, 1933
Married May 11, 1957
Divorced August 26, 1977

Robert Ames
Born March 15, 1932
Married May 11, 1957
Divorced August 26, 1977

Joe Ames
Born February 2, 1930
Married June 18, 1955

Claire Jansen
Born July 18, 1932
Married June 18, 1955

Sam Ames
Born May 18, 1958

Skylar Ames
Born June 22, 1963

Grace Ames
Born October 5, 1958

Chapter 1
Skylar
July 3, 1976
5 a.m.

Today is the day when maybe Skye will be kissed for the first time. By Zack. She hopes. At least she can dream.

Skye wants to write in her journal. She couldn't sleep. It was so hot last night, and besides, she's too excited about this weekend, the Fourth of July Bicentennial weekend.

Skye stands at her bedroom window as the sun rises over Lake Michigan. It is barely daybreak, and the air is already warm. Her oversized Camp Whispering Pines T-shirt, which she bought at camp last year and wears as a nightshirt, is damp with sweat and sticks to her back. She starts writing in the blue spiral notebook laid flat on the windowsill.

The sun is coming up over the lake. The best part of living on Lakeview Street is seeing the sun rise over Lake Michigan. Dad says people in California would pay a lot of money for a view like this.

She chews on the end of her pen and stares at her neat, backhanded cursive.

Lake Michigan is quiet and smooth and flat, kind of like blue silk with bits of orange and gold

This is good. She likes this description and adds *from the rising sun.*

This morning, Zack, Billy, Jenny, and I are going to film more of our Declaration of Independence movie project for our summer honors class. We have to get it done soon because our class will present all projects at the Bicentennial History Student Fair on August 2, the day John Hancock signed the declaration.

After lunch, Grandma Kitty is coming over to spend the afternoon, and then Great-uncle Chester and Grandma Edna and Uncle Rob will come over to watch the fireworks, and maybe Aunt Vivian will drive from Milwaukee, too.

She sets down her pen and closes the notebook. That's enough for now. What she didn't write in her journal—what she hopes will maybe happen, but doesn't even dare write down, or tell anyone, not even Jenny, *especially* not Jenny, is that maybe Zack will kiss her. Or even if he doesn't kiss her, maybe he will look at her as a girl he *likes*, not just as his friend from their summer school Honors American History class. She's not exactly sure how this might happen, this kiss, but she imagines what it would feel like if it does. They will be talking about—well, something— and Zack will lean toward her, and then their lips will touch, and she'll feel like she's melting inside, just like it says in romance novels.

Skye closes her notebook, slips it into the top drawer of her desk, and flops down on her bed. She just turned thirteen two weeks ago, but she is sure when she is eighty years old—in 2043, a completely different century—she will remember this day.

"Maybe you could go for just one semester," Ben says.

Grace and Ben are lying on a plaid wool blanket, looking up at the fading stars as the sky lightens from ink to pale violet. They have been at Big Beach all night, roasting marshmallows, drinking beer, and hanging out with friends.

The beach's real name is Middleport Municipal Beach, but everyone calls it Big Beach. It's a magnificent crescent of smooth sand stretching a quarter mile along the shore of Lake Michigan, protected by grassy bluffs leading up to Overlook Drive. The beach closes at 10 p.m., but this weekend, Bicentennial weekend, the beach is unofficially open all night. Every half hour or so a police car drives slowly along the road behind the beach. "Be careful. Make sure those fires are out. Happy Fourth!" the officers call out as they pass.

Blankets and tents dot the sand, and a few campfires still flicker along the beach. The scent of sulfur and smoke, mixed with the occasional whiff of pot, wafts across the sand.

Farther down the beach, a couple of guys are lighting fireworks that hiss and pop and burst into a confetti of light.

Someone yells, "Happy Fourth of July," and someone calls back, "It's not the Fourth of July yet, dork."

Grace touches her thumb to the ring encircling her right ring finger. It's a pink tourmaline, her birthstone, set in a slim gold band. It's not an engagement ring, exactly, but rather a ring Ben gave her because they love each other and have talked about getting married after they graduate from college. Her junior year abroad is starting in two months, however—nine months in Aix-en-Provence—and it has become a wall between them. They've talked for weeks with no resolution, going around and around in a conversation circle, just like the ring she wears.

She sometimes wishes she had never applied for her junior year abroad, had tossed the application in the trash when her French literature professor had handed her the form and said tartly, "Grace, apply! Your French is good, but it can get better. You *must* go to France." But she did apply, and deep down, she's glad.

"I'm supposed to go for a whole school year," Grace says. "That's how the program works."

"You should go. It's a once-in-a-lifetime opportunity," Ben says after a moment. He takes her hand and kisses it. "But I'll sure miss you."

Grace feels herself, yet again, wavering about her decision. She loves Ben, she really does. She loves his warm brown eyes, his easygoing personality, his gentleness with her family's dog Honey, and the way he laughs at old *Three Stooges* comedies on TV. He says he fell in love with her in eleventh-grade chemistry lab when he asked her if Moe, Larry, Curly, or Shemp was her favorite, never expecting she'd respond, because, he told her later, most girls hated the Stooges. But she had watched reruns of the films on TV for years with her great-uncle Chester, and she had replied, "There's only one answer: Shemp, of course." She loves the way Ben's light brown hair always looks tousled, no matter how much he combs it, and the goofy way he bowls, throwing the ball awkwardly so it bounces along the gutter like a pinball, and she loves how he brings her a homemade brownie every Saturday from his parents' restaurant, McLaren's Pub and Grill. Yes, she loves him, and the thought of not seeing him for nine months makes her ache.

But . . . she wants to go to Aix-en-Provence. She wants to practice her French with real French people instead of speaking into a microphone in the language lab. She wants to walk along cobblestoned streets, browse through markets on Saturday morning, sniff the fragrance of lavender fields, and see the café in Arles where Van Gogh drank coffee. She can't, won't, give that up. Is she selfish like her best friend Heidi says she is? Grace suspects Heidi maybe is jealous of her relationship with Ben because Heidi's boyfriend Hank is kind of a jerk who bosses her around. But she doesn't want to look back twenty years from now and regret that she gave up the opportunity to spend a year in France.

She imagines two versions of her future self. One is married to Ben. That future Grace has never been to Europe. She says to her future daughter or son, "I could have spent a year in France, but I couldn't leave your father." Her other future self is not married to Ben. She's married to some other man who is a blur in her imagination, or maybe she's married to no one at all. This future self looks at a faded Polaroid of Ben and her together, smiling, arms wrapped around each other, and thinks, "I still love him." Neither vision satisfies. She abruptly sits up and brushes sand off her legs.

"What's wrong?" Ben asks.

She shrugs. "Nothing."

When in an awkward pause in a conversation, look at Lake Michigan. Grace doesn't know where the thought comes from, but it works. The sun pokes over the horizon, spooling ribbons of colors across the smooth surface of the water. In the bushes clinging to the bluff bordering the beach, the doves begin their morning song, and red-winged blackbirds dart among the bushes.

"Let's talk about this later, okay? It's almost the Bicentennial." She kisses him. "This is a weekend to have fun. Today we're together and that's all that matters."

She kisses him on the cheek. "Happy almost Bicentennial, Ben."

"Happy almost Bicentennial, Grace," Ben says, sadly.

The front door squeaks as it opens. Honey scrambles to her feet and runs down the hallway, toenails clicking on the wood floor. Then the sound of Grace and Ben murmuring their good-byes.

Claire listens for her daughter's' footsteps in the hallway and calls out, "Did you have a good time?"

A pause.

"It was fun. A lot of people we knew were there."

"How's Ben?"

Another pause.

"He's fine."

"Get some rest now, sweetie."

"Okay, Mom. Talk to you later."

The bathroom door closes, followed by the sound of water running. Claire sighs and shifts in bed, trying to find one spot that isn't damp with sweat. Joe snores beside her, blissfully unperturbed, his tall, sturdy body sprawled across the mattress. While it exasperates her that he's not bothered by the heat and humidity, she's glad he's sleeping. He's exhausted. The three-hour round-trip drive to work in Sheboygan and back is wearing him down. Every week he seems more faded, like a shirt that's gone through the wash too many times. It's hard to believe that on the Fourth of July two years ago they were celebrating his new job as an engineering supervisor at Chatham Industries. Then, six months later, the recession, the layoffs, and Joe sitting at the dining room table day after day circling job ads with a red marker and mailing resumes to one company after another, knowing many of them were unlikely to hire a forty-six-year-old engineer when there was a glut of eager young engineers to pick from. Finally, after four months, the offer from A&H Milk Processing, and the grueling drive five days a week.

She flops over, trying to find a cool spot on the sheet. She will bring up the topic of air conditioning with Joe again next week, after the Bicentennial weekend, and insist they install an air conditioner before next summer using the money she's saved from her part-time job at the library. She doesn't understand why he stubbornly resists it. The lake breeze is refreshing, but it's not enough on days like this, when it's sticky by 6 a.m.

Her thoughts drift back to Grace. She'll talk with her after the weekend. She's not sure what she should say to her eldest daughter. She is happy that Grace has this opportunity to spend a year in France, as much as she will miss her and worry about her so far away. Grace loves Ben, Claire is sure of that, and he's a thoughtful and steady young man who loves Grace. He wants to be a veterinarian, and Ben reminds Claire of a loyal, gentle labrador retriever. Is Grace throwing something wonderful away? When you're young, Claire muses, you think love like that can come along again, but sometimes it doesn't.

Perhaps Claire is being selfish. If Grace should fall in love with a French man—and Claire is sure her pretty, poised, blonde-haired daughter will catch the eye of one or more suave French men while she's in Aix-en-Provence—Grace might very well end up living 4,000 miles away across an ocean with children who speak French and who will think of Grandfather and Grandmother Ames as the strange Americans who visit once a year, and she can't bear to think of that possibility.

Or perhaps—the thought comes to her suddenly as she rolls over to the edge of the mattress futilely seeking a cool spot—maybe her anxiety about Grace's year abroad comes from someplace else entirely, someplace deeper. Perhaps it's anger at that entire damn continent where Mike died that is at the root of her tangled feelings.

Mike. He'd be fifty-two now. Odd to think that. How would he have aged? She tries to imagine her brother with thin, graying hair brushed back above a creased forehead, stooped shoulders, perhaps a paunch, but she simply can't picture him that way.

He remains frozen in her memory as he was the last time she saw Mike, slim and tall and fair-haired like their father, hugging her good-bye at the train station. "Be good, kiddo," he had said. "Next time I see you, I bet you're going to be all grown up, a young lady."

She wonders, as she has for thirty years, if Mike would have followed in their father's footsteps and become a pharmacist. Would Mike have married Maggie, or would she have tossed him over for Greg? Or would Mike have met a sweet English bride while he was stationed in Great Britain? Would Jansen's Pharmacy still exist? What nieces and nephews might she have had?

She has thought about these questions for thirty years, but questions are all they will ever be. *Oh, Mike.* She turns her thoughts to today. Joe had wanted to throw a big Fourth of July party this year like they did last year, and invite her snooty cousins from Illinois like they did last year. He loves to show off their view of Lake Michigan.

"Your cousins may have their big houses and country clubs, but they don't have that, dear," Joe tells her, gesturing out the window at Lake Michigan whenever she relays the news from Alice about their trip to Italy or Arthur's new Cadillac.

She had put her foot down this year and said, *No, they weren't going to host a party this year.* She told Joe that she wanted to enjoy this Bicentennial Fourth and watch the Tall Ships as they glided past the Statue of Liberty on television instead of spending all day serving drinks and waiting on guests. They had compromised on inviting just Mom, Claire's uncle Chester, and Joe's mother Edna, who is married to Chester, which makes her mother-in-law her aunt by marriage. Although she'd never admit it to Joe, she's never cared for his unmaternal mother and can't understand what sweet Uncle Chester ever saw in Edna, unless, she supposes, it was sex, or simply some excitement injected into her shy uncle's life when he started dating Joe's divorced, carefree mother. Joe's brother Rob will also join the family to watch the Bicentennial Eve fireworks, and perhaps Vivian will drive down from Milwaukee as well.

She glances at the alarm clock. Nearly 7 a.m. She tosses back the sheet, rolls out of bed, slips on her pink cotton duster, which gapes between the snaps, and slides her feet into her pink terrycloth slippers. Up until age forty, her weight was a trim 115 pounds at 5'4" and she never had to fret about her figure like her friend Betty always did, but in the past four years she's gained and lost the same ten pounds, and each time it's getting harder to lose. She opens the bedroom door and Honey scrambles to her feet, pom-pom tail wagging like a metronome. Honey trots to the kitchen door. Claire lets her out and watches as the brown miniature poodle sniffs the grass, searches for a spot, squats, and does her business. Honey kicks her hind legs when she's done and runs happily back to the door, ready for breakfast.

Sometimes Claire thinks that it would be lovely to be a pampered little poodle with nothing to do but run and play and eat all day with no worries about a husband driving so far to a stressful job, no older daughter flying across the ocean to live in a foreign country for nine months, no teenaged daughter mooning over a wild boy, and no elderly mother insisting on living alone in a house that's too big for her to manage.

She opens the door to let Honey back inside, fills her bowl with kibble, and makes coffee in the Mr. Coffee automatic drip machine that the girls gave her for Christmas. Joe has never warmed to it. He grumbles that there's nothing like the taste of coffee made the old-fashioned way, but Claire thinks the automatic drip coffee is marvelously mild, not bitter like coffee boiled in a stainless-steel percolator. She wonders if it's not the coffee he misses, but what it represents: his Grandmother Ames's home with coffee bubbling on the stove and the safety they found after the family moved in and Joe and his brother Rob finally had stability.

She pours herself a cup of coffee and sits down at the kitchen table. This is her favorite part of the day: sitting quietly before the chaos begins and she's tugged in a dozen different directions. Later this morning she'll meet Betty and Alma for this month's meeting of the Art and Book Club. They decided to meet on the Bicentennial weekend, something that caused no end of friction with a few of the husbands, particularly Betty's Ed, who can be a curmudgeon, and then she'll come back home to prepare for tonight. Although only five people are coming this evening, she still needs to make appetizers, scrub the bathroom, vacuum the living room rug, dust the wicker furniture on the porch, hang red-white-and-blue bunting beneath the front window, and decorate the yard with miniature flags.

Men simply don't *understand*, she thinks, as she drinks the last of her coffee. Joe is tidy, but he doesn't grasp that cleaning is more than wiping away grime. It is crisply ironed sheets, grooves in freshly vacuumed rugs, neatly stacked magazines on the coffee table. It takes work to keep a home sparkling, work that she knows Joe and the girls don't fully appreciate, but she isn't quite ready to do what Betty has urged the girls in the club to do, which is to accept wrinkled clothes and messy closets so they can spend more time *finding themselves*, whatever that means.

Betty's embrace of feminism came as a surprise. The first time she met Betty was at a PTA meeting when Grace was in first grade. Betty came dressed in a pink houndstooth suit and a pillbox hat, inspired by

Jackie Kennedy, Claire had assumed, even though Betty, with her lively intelligent eyes and direct manner, reminds her more of Eleanor Roosevelt.

Three years ago, Betty read *The Feminine Mystique* after Ed had his affair with his secretary. Betty forgave Ed eventually, but since then she's turned into a feminist and even subscribes to *Ms.* magazine.

Find herself. Claire doesn't even know where to begin to look to find the girl she had been, the girl who loved watercolor painting, singing in the school choir, and tilting her head back on rainy April afternoons to feel the drops splash on her face, the girl she almost forgot had ever existed once she became a wife, and soon after, a mother.

Well, no time to think of that now when there's so much to do. She sits for a moment, savoring the peace and quiet before her busy day begins.

Chapter 4
Joe
7 a.m.

Joe is still half asleep, but he hears Claire padding about the bedroom. The closet door slides open, and he hears the click of hangers, and smells a whiff of the Jean Naté cologne she loves to spritz on after a bath or shower, a citrusy scent that he finds incredibly sexy.

"Morning, Joe," Claire says.

Joe grunts and burrows his head under the pillow. He has never outgrown his love of sleeping in, but he knows he must get up. He's a man with responsibilities, and he can't sleep all morning like his girls do, curled in a tangle of sheets until noon. He'd like to get a jog in before he starts his chores and errands, but he probably won't have time. He started jogging last month after he noticed that he had developed a paunch and was panting by the time he got to the green on the third hole at Middleport Golf Course. His new exercise routine alarms Claire, who is convinced he'll drop over from a heart attack, just like her father and his father, but Dr. Keenan says his heart is sound and encourages him to exercise.

He's glad they aren't hosting Claire's Illinois cousins after all. He enjoys getting together, despite her cousins' constant bragging about their country club memberships and European vacations. He and Rob never had much of a family life, and it's important for the girls to stay connected to their cousins. But Claire was right. It's better not to have the pressure of grilling burgers, mixing drinks, and cleaning up for hours afterwards. They can watch the fireworks tonight, and tomorrow they'll enjoy the parade and watch the second fireworks. Personally, he thinks it's a waste of money for the city to have fireworks two nights in a row, but Claire said America only turns two hundred years old once, so the city should do something special.

This weekend will be more like the Fourth of July celebrations they enjoyed when he and Claire were dating, like the summer he stayed in Madison working at the engineering library and taking a summer course in thermodynamics. At the time, he couldn't believe that he was actually in college—him, the son of a man who dropped out of school after eighth grade—but thanks to serving three years in the Air Force as a mechanic and the G.I. Bill, there he was at the university studying electrical engineering.

Claire came to Madison for the weekend and stayed with his roommate's girlfriend. How odd that Claire stayed elsewhere, when young couples live openly together now and don't care what anyone thinks. Even Grace, when they call her at school, casually remarks that she's spending the night with Ben, which he thinks is far too much information for a father to handle. On that Fourth back in 1955, he and his roommate Tom hosted a barbecue for their circle of friends. They sat in the backyard at the house where he and Tom rented the top-floor flat, drinking bottles of Schlitz and eating hamburgers and corn on the cob. The memory is so vivid he can almost taste the buttery, salty kernels and smell the sizzling burgers. He had a secondhand hi-fi, and he and Claire and Tom and Jane had danced to Glenn Miller as the sky darkened to a purply haze. Later that night, Tom and Jane went to a party, while he and Claire sat on the porch swing necking, and he slid his hand along her thigh . . .

The alarm clock jangles him from his reverie. His wife is standing next to him, already dressed in blue pedal pushers and a crisp red and white gingham shirt, with a blue headband around her smooth blond hair, still beautiful at forty-four.

Come back to bed with me, my love, he wants to say. *We'll make love and sleep till noon.*

But they have children and chores and company coming today. He grunts.

Claire smiles, "Why so grumpy? It's a beautiful morning!"

"Too early."

"I've been up for an hour already," she says lightly.

She's right. She's already been hard at work while he's still a slug in bed. He sits up, wraps his arms around his wife, and kisses her on the cheek, aware of his stale morning breath. She pats his shoulder and holds out a powder-blue polo shirt. "Why don't you wear this today? It's fresh from the laundry, and it matches your eyes." she says.

He nods and rolls out of bed, wistfully releasing the memory of July 4, 1955. It's July 3, 1976, with much to do this day and no time to lie in bed and make love to his wife.

Chapter 5
Vivian
8 a.m.

"More coffee?" Greg asks.

Vivian and Greg are sitting at the green metal bistro table on the flagstone patio in Vivian's backyard. She had bought the clapboard bungalow on the East Side of Milwaukee, a block from the lake, ten years ago. What an ordeal that was! Three banks had turned her down before she found one willing to approve a mortgage to a "spinster" as she was listed on the application. She loves her small, airy home. Greg made breakfast while she was still asleep: scrambled eggs, deliciously light and fluffy, buttered toast, and a blue carafe filled with hot coffee.

Vivian nods. "Yes, thank you."

Greg refills Vivian's mug, yellow ceramic with sunflowers painted on it, her favorite, one that she bought at a farmers' market in France years ago.

"These eggs are wonderful," she adds. "Whenever I try making scrambled eggs, which isn't often, they're always runny. I've always been helpless in the kitchen, much to Mom's despair."

Greg smiles. "Your mom was—and still is, I'm sure—a great cook. I remember all those dinners at your parents' house, the roast beef and mashed potatoes she'd serve every Sunday. And her apple pie! In Guam, I dreamed about her pie."

"Your mother was an excellent cook, too," Vivian says.

Greg nods. "Yes, she was. But the dinners at your parents' house were always special."

They are quiet for a moment. Vivian studies his face. He's fifty-two now, and thirty-four years have passed since he was her high school sweetheart. His lean face is creased around his eyes and mouth, and his brown hair is streaked with gray, but he is still a handsome man, one with kindness in his gray eyes. Greg was always gracious. Even when he saw her for the first time after he returned home following his service as a Navy medic in Guam—a little more than a year after she sent him that awful Dear John letter— he was kind. They had run into each other in front of Dillworth's on the Saturday before Christmas in December 1945. She had taken the train up from Chicago to Middleport to spend the holiday with her family and was running errands for her mother. They had literally bumped into each other on the sidewalk in front of the five-and-dime store. *Greg*, she had said. *I'm glad you're back. How are you*? He had nodded and said, *I'm fine.* They had stood on the sidewalk for a moment, silence between them, and then she had said, *About the letter—it seemed for the best.* He had nodded, touched her arm, and said, *No need to say anymore. I understand. All the best to you, Red.* But she saw the hurt in his eyes and knew she had wounded him terribly, and she wished for months afterward that she had followed him and said she was sorry, instead of standing there on the sidewalk, holding her bag of candy canes and tinsel as he walked away.

They have seen each other seven times in the past three weeks since Greg called and said he had moved back to Wisconsin to be closer to his daughter, who had attended Northwestern University, fell in love, married, and now lives with her husband in Chicago. "Close, but not too close," he said with a smile. He sold his optometry practice in Santa Rosa and bought a practice from a retiring optometrist in Milwaukee, and he commutes one day a week to Chicago to teach at the optometry school there.

He called Vivian a week after he moved back. First lunch, all light conversation and catching up over Caesar salads with no mention of the past. Then, drinks at a cozy place downtown and more pleasant conversation, with brief forays into the past with reminiscences about their childhood and Mike. A few days later, dinner and conversation shifted back to the present. A few more movies and dinners and then last night, a movie and a nightcap and unexpectedly, and delightfully, a night together.

Yet they have not broached the subject of their broken engagement. They've gotten it backwards, Vivian thinks: first sex, and then the conversation, but wasn't everything jumbled these days? All those norms and "what will people think" that she and her peers agonized over vanished like a puff of smoke in the haze of the sixties, and young adults no longer cared what anyone thought. They did what they wanted, and good for them.

"When did you learn to cook?" Vivian says to change the subject and ease them past this awkward moment.

He smiles. "College. An endless diet of peanut butter and jelly sandwiches got old fast, so when I moved into an apartment I learned to cook fast. I can only manage the basics, though—hamburgers, spaghetti, things like that."

"And then when Maggie . . ." he pauses, and she sees the pang of grief in his eyes. He glances away, looks at the yard for a moment, and then turns his gaze back to her.

"When Maggie got sick," he continues, "I started doing most of the cooking. Most of the time she didn't have an appetite, but sometimes I could coax her to eat a little something."

"Maggie was lucky to have you. You were a devoted husband."

"I was lucky to have her." Greg says simply. "She was a wonderful wife and mother."

"Maggie was always sweet. I'm—I'm glad you found happiness, Greg. I truly am," Vivian says.

"Thank you, Vivian," Greg replies. He reaches across the table and takes her hand.

They are quiet for a moment. Vivian watches a fat robin hop across the lawn and she closes her eyes, leans back, and feels the sun on her face. It was a beautiful morning and being here with Greg made it even better. She's amazed that this is happening, that Greg is back in her life, and she feels gratified and at ease with him. And yet, the broken engagement hovers over their time together like a faint mist that needs to be cleared from the air.

She opens her eyes. Greg is still holding her hand and looking at her with that clear, straightforward gaze she remembers from high school.

"I—" Vivian says. She pauses to collect her thoughts. She takes a deep breath, hesitates. *Oh, the hell with it. Better to rip off the bandage and get to it.*

"Greg. We've been avoiding the past so far, but I'm so sorry about what I did. I never meant to hurt you."

He nods. She sees a flicker of pain in his eyes.

He glances down, and with his free hand he traces his finger across the metal table and looks back at her.

"I loved you, Red," he says quietly, using the nickname he called her in high school because of her auburn hair. "It took a long time to understand why you broke it off."

"Greg, it wasn't you. Please believe that. It was *me*. I needed to get away."

She takes a sip of coffee to gather her thoughts and then plunges ahead. "After Mike died, I had to get away, do something different."

He nods.

"I was terribly selfish, I know that now," Vivian says. "Claire was only twelve. I left her and my parents alone with their grief, and I walked away. From the sadness, from the uncertainty, from you. I'm so terribly sorry, Greg."

He squeezes her hand.

"Vivian, don't be so hard on yourself. You were nineteen and grieving. Moving to Chicago was perhaps what you needed."

"But that's not what people were supposed to *do*!" Vivian cries "We were supposed to simply get on with it, with life."

Greg shrugs. "Last I heard, Congress never passed a law mandating that every American push down their emotions and just get on with it after the war."

"*You* did."

He shakes his head. "Not really. I had to get away, too. A fresh start." He releases her hand and busies himself by spreading strawberry jam on his toast.

"We all grieve in our own way, and we were so young. Younger than my daughter Alison is now," he adds quietly. "And it all worked out—Maggie and I had a long, fine life together. And it seems like you've had a good life, too."

"I can't complain. I have an interesting career and good friends and—" she takes a breath "—a few romances along the way."

He nods, his expression neutral.

"But not many men are interested in an independent career woman who speaks her mind," she adds.

"Your feistiness was one of the things I loved about you," he says, smiling. "When you were working on the high school paper, you were the only girl writing about sports. Vivian Jansen, girl sports reporter, it said in the yearbook."

"It was more interesting than writing about the home-economics class teas," she laughs. "And now that you're back in Milwaukee," she adds lightly to ease them back to less fraught territory, "you don't miss California at all?"

He takes a bite of toast, swallows, and answers. "California was like paradise in the years after the war, but it's getting crowded and expensive, and, more importantly, Alison is here, and my sisters and their families."

"Another fresh start. Closing the circle as it were?"

He takes her hand again. "Yes, I hope so. And what about you?

"What about me?" She's not sure what he's referring to.

"A fresh start. Are you looking for a fresh start? Or are you happy with the way things are?"

Vivian thinks for a moment before answering.

"I love my life," Vivian says cautiously. "I enjoy my work, I have friends, I travel, and I can eat ice cream for dinner if I want."

He nods, and she detects a trace of disappointment in his face.

"And yet," she adds quickly. "It does gets old sometimes. The same cocktail parties and luncheons again and again. Writing the same advertising copy and press releases for my clients. I think to myself, do I still want to be doing the same old, same old when I'm sixty? Isn't there more to life? And even eating ice cream for dinner while sitting on the couch watching *All in the Family* gets old after a while. So, yes, it may be time for something—or someone new." She feels herself blush.

Greg smiles, that sweet slow smile that she remembers so well from high school. "Possibly someone to go to a movie with on a Saturday night?"

That sounds lovely to Vivian.

She smiles. "Possibly."

He lifts his coffee mug and toasts her. "To the slow road of possibility then."

She raises her coffee mug in return. "The slow road of possibility."

They are quiet for a moment. The breeze stirs the leaves on the oak tree. Robins and sparrows twitter in the branches and a cardinal whistles and chirps and soars across the yard in a blur of red. She watches a squirrel scamper along the wood fence and leap into the branches of a neighboring maple tree.

She had been dithering about asking him, worrying it was too soon and what it might imply, but she decides to take the chance.

"You mentioned that Alison and David are spending the weekend at the beach and your sister and her family are spending the week at their lake house in northern Wisconsin," she says.

"Too many mosquitoes for me," he says, still smiling.

She takes a deep breath. She has navigated life on her own terms for thirty years and dated many interesting men, yet she feels suddenly shy now with this man she kissed last when she was in the tenth grade.

"Would you like to come with me to Claire and Joe's this evening to watch the fireworks?"

His smile broadens into a grin, and he kisses her hand. "Yes, my dear, I would."

Kitty reaches for her handbag and peers inside to check the contents once more. Ticket, wallet, traveler checks—yes, it's all there. Her pink Samsonite suitcase packed with three cotton shifts, three blouses, two cardigans, white canvas Keds, leather lace-up walking shoes, two pairs of denim dungarees, elastic-waist blue Bermuda shorts, socks, underwear, stockings, cotton nightgown and robe, and slippers is set by the back door.

In seven hours, she will be on a plane to Denver and the start of a two-month automobile trip through Colorado, Utah, Arizona, Wyoming, and Montana, and that, she thinks, is cause for a bit of celebration. She grips the edge of the table for support and gingerly stands up, painfully aware of her arthritis. She worries that exploring the parks may be challenging with her creaky knees, but she is bringing her cane and good walking shoes and, arthritis or no arthritis, she's going on this trip. She fetches a glass tumbler from the kitchen cupboard, retrieves the bottle of brandy from the cherrywood cabinet drawer in the dining room, and pours a splash in the glass.

Frederick loved his brandy old-fashioneds; she doesn't really like the taste of brandy, or any hard liquor, in fact, but the brandy will boost her courage.

Claire would be horrified if she knew her mother was sipping brandy at 9:30 a.m. Vivian . . . well, Vivian would pretend to be shocked, but Kitty suspects her oldest daughter likely has taken the hair-of-the-dog cure more than once. After all, it's a special day that calls for a little celebration. At 3:30 p.m. she is going to board an airplane for only the third time in her life on her way to do what she had wanted to do since she was a Girl Scout in 1914, going on hikes, learning to tie a dozen different knots, and sitting around a campfire singing cowboy songs and listening to Miss Adams, their troop leader, telling them stories about growing up in the wilds of Montana in the 1880s.

Claire and Joe and Vivian—or maybe not Vivian, for she thinks Vivian is the only one who might understand—will think Kitty has lost her mind when they find out, but she can't worry about that now, or she'll never have the nerve to go. She glances at the letter she placed on the corner of the kitchen table, where they will be sure to see it.

I'm off on a little trip with Agnes. We're going to explore some of the national parks . . . the Grand Canyon, Yosemite, Yellowstone, and Glacier. Don't worry, we'll be perfectly fine! We've made our hotel reservations along the way, our route is mapped out, and Agnes belongs to the AAA Motor Club. Her son lives near Denver, and we will call him collect every night from our hotel. I will call you at least twice a week. I am bringing a bag of quarters as well as a roll of stamps and plenty of notecards and envelopes.

I'm sorry I didn't tell you beforehand, but I know you worry and would have tried to talk me out of it. Vivian and Claire, this is something your old mother very much wants to do. It's something Agnes and I have talked about since we were girls. Please be happy for me as I embark on my little adventure.

She imagines Claire reading the letter, shaking her head, and handing it to Joe and saying, *Whatever possessed her to do it? It's not safe for two old ladies to drive around on their own.*

Kitty suspects Claire will use her summer adventure as one more reason to prod her to sell the house and to move into a one-bedroom at Sunrise Senior Apartments. *Why do they call it Sunrise?* she wonders. Sunset would be more appropriate. The girls have been pushing her to sell the house since Frederick died sixteen years ago, with Claire pushing the hardest. Kitty suspects that Vivian isn't pressing her as hard to move because, as a spinster of fifty-one, she isn't too far off herself from the age when people will push *her* to sell her house and move into an apartment.

But Kitty isn't ready and won't be for some time. She and Frederick moved into the house at 303 Maple Street in 1931. It was during the Great Depression, but Frederick owned his own drugstore on Main Street, and they had carefully saved the money for their home. They were fortunate Frederick was a pharmacist and owned his own store. Even during the hard times, people still needed aspirin, bandages, and soap, and children still saved their pennies for ice cream sodas.

They had raised three children in the brick two-story house on Maple Street. It was where Mike had grown up. The chalk marks that Frederick made to record the children's height every year are still faintly visible on the basement wall. Mike's toy blocks are still stacked on the basement shelves, the cardboard box covered in dust. There's a splotch of blue paint on the back patio that Mike spilled when he was painting his toy sailboat. Once the house is sold, those reminders of Mike's childhood will be lost forever.

Kitty walks into the living room to check that the windows are shut and fastened firmly, and the pale green damask drapes partially drawn. She glances at their silver-framed wedding picture on the cream-colored fireplace mantel. In the picture, Frederick is tall and lean and fair-haired (she always thought he looked a bit like Douglas Fairbanks), his arm curled protectively around her waist, and she's petite and slim with chin-length bobbed hair that had just become fashionable (her hair was a deep auburn then, although the color doesn't show in the black-and-white photo) wearing a knee-length ivory gown and veil, holding a bouquet of white roses, looking up at Frederick, smiling at her thoughtful and handsome husband.

Next to that picture is one of the entire family that was taken in early December 1941. December 6, in fact. She and Frederick are standing by the Christmas tree, which they had put up that very day. Mike is next to Frederick, taller than him by an inch, and Vivian and Claire are kneeling in front, both wearing angora sweater sets and plaid skirts. Their neighbors, Emma and Harry, stopped in to say hello (oh, she missed how people used to simply drop in to visit!) and Frederick fetched his camera from the closet, handed it to Harry, and asked him to snap a picture. It turned out to be one of her favorite family photos. All of them smiling—Mike a handsome high school senior, Vivian a beautiful teenager, Claire a nine-year-old in pigtails. They were so happy that day, oblivious, like most Americans were, of what was ahead of them—and what was ahead for Mike—and what would never be ahead for him . . . a wedding, children, and grandchildren and . . .

She presses her lips together, turns away from that family picture, and looks again at her wedding photo.

Fifty-six years later, she still remembers the details of their first date on July 4, 1920. She was eighteen and had walked into the drugstore two days earlier to purchase aspirin powder for her mother and there he was, the new young assistant pharmacist from Milwaukee. She was going steady with Ned Callahan at the time, an easygoing chatterbox of a boy who lived across the street. But when she spotted Frederick standing behind the counter, smiling at her, blue eyes twinkling, she knew, she just *knew* that he was the one for her. He asked her if she'd like to meet for an ice cream sundae on Independence Day. She had said yes, and they had talked for an hour at the ice cream parlor and then taken a stroll, and then she had invited him for Sunday dinner the next week and, well, that was that. She broke things off with Ned the next day, who swore he'd never find another girl. But within a week he was going steady with someone new. As for her and Frederick, they married a month after their first date, and despite her mother's tart reminder of the saying, "marry in haste, repent in leisure," they had shared forty happy years together.

Oh, she and Frederick had fun together in those early years. Frederick worked long, hard hours in the drugstore that he bought from Doc Reynolds. Still, they managed to shoehorn fun in. They had picnics in the park and spent afternoons at the beach. They took long drives in their Buick, motoring to Lake Geneva or Milwaukee, and sometimes to Madison. They went to the movies at the Neapolitan Theater on Sunday afternoons. They rented a cottage near Eagle River for two weeks every summer. They went to parties with their neighbors and friends and played records on the gramophone or listened to music on the radio while drinking bottles of beer and root beer that had been set out in tin buckets filled with ice, and they ate tomato and cheese sandwiches and apple pie. It was a joy simply to be together, to let loose their worries during the hard years of the Great Depression.

After the children were born, they took them along to picnics and hayrides and sledding in the park. Simple things that made so many happy memories.

No. She's not selling her house until she's too frail to climb the stairs to her bedroom. And before she reaches that stage, she's going to see a bit of America, just like she and Agnes dreamed about when they were twelve-year-old Girl Scouts leafing through an atlas together, pointing out the places they wanted to explore.

Chapter 7
Joe
10 a.m.

It's only 10 a.m., but it seems later to Joe. He's had his toast and coffee, cut the grass, gone for a quick jog after Claire's protests that it was too hot, and then took a long shower. He walks in the kitchen, wearing the blue polo shirt and khaki shorts that Claire had suggested. She's sitting at the kitchen table with a pad of paper in front of her. She taps the pencil against the table, thinking, and jots a note on the pad, then looks up and smiles when she sees him.

He kisses her shoulder. She absently pats his hand. "Hmm, you smell nice. Thank you for cutting the grass, sweetheart."

"Of course. Now what do you want me to do?"

He's been trying to be extra helpful since last week and The Great Casserole Dish Incident, as he's begun to think of it. It was a stupid argument. He was exhausted that night after the long drive from work, the heavy traffic, the humidity. After a late dinner—Claire had warmed up stuffed shells with marinara sauce—he became obstinate about scrubbing the damn casserole dish crusted with dried tomato sauce and bits of pasta. They went to bed angry at each other, the pan moldering in the sink. He dozed fitfully, and waking at 1 a.m., discovered Claire was not in bed. He found her in the kitchen standing at the sink, scrubbing the dish. He silently took the sponge from her hand and finished the job. She had touched his shoulder, gone back to bed, and said no more about it.

But he knew something was bothering her, a dissatisfaction, a restlessness. Even her part-time job at the library, ten hours a week, that he had encouraged her to apply for three years ago to give her something to do when the girls didn't need her as much, didn't seem to be enough. *What was it that women wanted?* After the instability of his own upbringing, he had vowed that he would be a good husband and provider, but it seems that is no longer enough for Claire, for all women in America now, in fact, with their talk of the Equal Rights Amendment and women's lib. Liberation from what, he's not sure. His mother had never seemed constrained by anything, certainly not by housework or caring for her sons.

"Joe, could you please call your mother and Uncle Chester and tell them to come about seven," Claire says. "Or we can pick them up; that might be easier."

He nods, steps over to the harvest-gold telephone hanging on the wall, and dials.

It rings, one, two, three times. He waits, knowing that Chester moves slowly now that he's nearly eighty.

"Hello?" He hears his mother's quavery voice on the other end.

"Mom! It's Joe."

"Who?

"*Joe.* Your son."

"Oh, Rob!"

"Not Rob, Mom. *Joe.*"

He hears a click as Chester picks up on the other line.

"Joe!" Chester's voice booms in the receiver. The first time Joe met Chester, he was startled that Claire's short, quiet uncle had a deep, sonorous voice, which he uses with relish as the baritone member of a barbershop quartet.

"Hello, Chester," Joe says. "Claire asked me to call to tell you to come over about seven tonight. We'll have some snacks and drinks and then watch the fireworks."

"We'll be there! Anything we can bring?"

"Only yourselves," Joe replies. "And I'll follow you home tonight and help you get Mom settled, or I can even pick you and Mom up."

"No need to do that," Chester replies crisply.

"It's no problem."

"Well . . . we'll see," Chester says. Joe understands. It's hard to accept help, and he wonders how he'll feel someday when Grace and Skye tell him that they'll drive *him* home.

"Well, good-bye now . . . uh, Joe," his mother says. He hears a clatter as his mother drops the phone.

"Dear, wait there!" Chester says. Then he adds in a whisper, "She's really not so bad today, not as bad as she seems on the phone, but we won't stay long."

"Good. See you tonight," Joe says.

He hangs up the phone and stares at it a minute, thinking of a Fourth of July long ago, in 1942 when he was twelve, the summer after the United States entered the war. They were in Grandmother Ames's backyard, celebrating with their cousins and a few neighbors. He remembers that his mother was wearing a red dress and sandals, her red-polished toes peeking through the straps, with her dark hair curled and pinned up in a Betty Grable-style do. She was leaning close to Elmer, the neighbor's son, who was home on leave, laughing and touching his chest, while Joe's sad sack of a father stood in the corner of the yard, gripping a beer bottle, staring down at the ground.

"Joe? You seem lost in thought," Claire says.

He shakes his head. "Mom's confused today."

"I'm sorry," Claire says. "I know it's hard for you." She walks over to hug him.

"It's not like she was ever Mother of the Year, but she used to be so full of life. And now she's just *there*."

"Thank goodness she has Chester," Claire says. "He's taking good care of her."

"I know." Joe nods. He tries to dismiss the worry about his mother from his mind. There's no use ruminating about it now, there's nothing he can do.

He turns to his wife and smiles. "Now, how about I go get the paper cups and napkins?"

Rob sits on the front stoop of his house drinking coffee from a chipped blue mug that says, "World's Best Dad," a Father's Day present from Sam ten years ago.

He likes to sit on the front porch because he can see a sliver of Lake Michigan, the poor man's ocean view, as he has told Amy many times. For twenty years of marriage, she has remained unimpressed. Nothing, not even a vivid blue lake eighty miles wide and three hundred miles long, can compare with her beloved Northwoods. And, he thinks sadly, in her mind he will never measure up to her old high school sweetheart, Dan, the one she had to leave behind when her family moved to Middleport.

It's been a month since she left for Rhinelander. Rob and Amy told Sam that she was going up north for a week to get Grandpa Frank settled in with the home nurse. She still isn't back. They both know, although they have not yet told Sam, that she might not come back, at least not for good. Sam is on a three-week biking trip through Iowa, Minnesota, and Wisconsin with two of his buddies. It was the boys' reward to themselves after they had spent a month with their Boy Scout troop painting benches and fire hydrants around town red, white, and blue in honor of the Bicentennial. Rob and Amy agreed in their last phone conversation three days ago that she will come home next week, after Sam returns, and they will sit down in the living room and tell him they are separating.

"We need a break, Rob," Amy had told him, resignation in her voice. "We both know it."

Damn it. Divorce. Rob hates that this will happen to Sam, even though he is eighteen and will be off to college next month. When their parents divorced, he was fifteen and Joe was seventeen. Thirty years later, the memory still stings. Mom did the right thing, he knows, because Dad couldn't keep a job and couldn't quit drinking, but he has never forgotten the pain, like a punch in the stomach, when his father walked out the door carrying his suitcase, his shoulders slumped. He had hugged him and Joe and said, "Boys, take care of your mother." Three years later he had a stroke at age fifty, dropping over while fueling a Chevrolet Deluxe at the gas station where he worked, and then lingering for six months before he died.

He turns his thoughts back to Amy and him. How had it happened, this crumbling of their marriage? They didn't yell and slam doors like Joe and Claire sometimes did. Neither of them had an affair, although he suspects that Amy and Dan, who had never married, and who Rob suspects always carried a torch for his wife, may have rekindled *something* or might start something the moment the ink is dry on the divorce papers.

No, he and Amy had simply drifted apart, like two leaves eddying along different currents. He remembers when he first saw her, standing in the corner at the school dance, looking like a shy fawn, skinny and long-legged with wispy brown hair falling in her eyes, and right then and there, in the Middleport High School gym, he was filled with a yearning to protect and care for her, which he has tried to do for twenty years. They were happy at first, he truly believes. Those first few years when he was studying for his teaching degree and they were living in that walk-up apartment on the East Side in Milwaukee. Then he was offered the job at Middleport High and became absorbed with teaching and coaching the high school boys baseball team. Sam came along and Amy focused on raising Sam and volunteering at the senior center. They grew apart. Yet maybe it was more than that: Amy had never adjusted to living here and never stopped pining for Up North.

Maybe he should have applied for a teaching job at one of the small high schools in northern Wisconsin all those years ago, as Amy had pushed him to do. He had argued that it would be crazy to give up his position at Middleport High and lose his years of seniority. But his resistance was due to something else as well, something he didn't tell Amy. He couldn't bear to live up there, surrounded by miles of forest, so far from Milwaukee. Some people found solace in rural places. He didn't. Whenever he and Amy would visit her parents, who had moved north after her father retired, he felt like he was drowning in the silence of the pine woods. The countryside reminded Rob of the years sitting alone in the house, his father gone and Joe working his pharmacy delivery route while Rob studied and waited for his mother or Joe to come home. Sometimes on those lonely evenings he'd walk to the library or the diner or the movie theater simply to be around people and hear conversation.

"Morning, Rob!"

The greeting jolts him out of his reverie, and he looks up and sees Lisa Anderson smiling at him. She's the new social studies and geography teacher at Middleport High, and she lives in a red bungalow on Charter Street. She's walking her Jack Russell terrier, Geo, short for geography. He doesn't know much about her, except that she's divorced, doesn't have any kids, and moved back to Wisconsin from Minnesota a year ago to be closer to her widowed mother. Rob's colleague Harriet, who has taught English composition for thirty years and is the faculty gossip, once remarked in the break room that Lisa's husband hadn't always been nice to her, *if you know what I mean*, and that Lisa's making a fresh start.

Even though he feels guilty looking at another woman as a still-married man, he can't help but notice that Lisa is an attractive woman, tall and slender with wide-set hazel eyes, coppery brown hair pulled up in a ponytail, and creamy skin with a smattering of freckles across her nose. She's wearing a white sleeveless blouse and blue denim shorts that reveal her long, tanned legs.

"Coming to brunch?"

"Brunch?" he says blankly.

"My pre-Fourth brunch? I sent you an invitation a few weeks ago?" She looks at him uncertainly.

"Oh, the brunch!" He says, suddenly remembering opening an invitation last week with red and blue stars and the words "Come to a Bicentennial Brunch!" printed on the front. He had tossed it in the garbage, then fished it out, and tacked it to the bulletin board in the kitchen, still clinging to the hope that Amy might return by the Fourth.

"Amy is still in Rhinelander," he says abruptly.

He's not even sure if he should be going to events without Amy. Can he go places without her before they've told Sam they're separating? Will people talk? Still, it's been him alone with the television news in the evening, just him and Walter Cronkite every night for the past month, punctuated once or twice a week by dinner with Claire and Joe. A social activity might do him some good.

"Oh. I'm sorry your father-in-law is still ill," Lisa says. Her forehead crinkles with worry, and he sees compassion in her eyes.

"He has heart failure. Amy is helping to set up the home care and get him settled in," Rob says. He feels like he is obligated to explain to people why Amy has been gone so long.

Lisa nods. "It always falls to the daughters, doesn't it?"

Not always, he thinks, remembering the months when he and Joe cared for Dad after his stroke. They were only eighteen and twenty. Joe took a leave from the army, and Rob dropped out of college for a semester. Their parents were divorced by then, and Mom was running around with that no-good bartender, and Dad's sisters were busy with their own families, so it was he and Joe who shouldered their father's care.

But he nods in agreement anyway because he knows she means well.

"But perhaps you can still come?" she asks. "Bring a guest if you'd like."

"I'll try."

"Uh, thanks" he adds.

Lisa gives him a quick smile, as though she worries that she somehow insulted him by inviting him to the party. He knows he must sound unfriendly, but he feels nervous because she's pretty and nice, and he's not sure how to navigate this invitation as a separated man.

Lisa waves goodbye, and he watches as she heads down the block, Geo trotting by her side, admiring her graceful walk.

Oh, hell, why not. He'll go over for a cup of coffee and a doughnut.

When Joe told Claire he was going to the store to pick up cups and napkins, Claire had suggested that he stop by Rob's house on the way to check on him. He's relieved she mentioned it; he is worried about his brother and wanted to drop in to see how he's doing, but he didn't want to suggest it himself because he figured Claire would prefer him to be around to help with the last-minute preparations for tonight.

"There are only four people coming, unlike like last year. I'm going to my book club anyway, so take the time to visit Rob," Claire told him.

Thank God they decided against entertaining the Illinois crowd this year. Claire was right. It is a weekend to enjoy, with all the festivities for the Bicentennial, instead of worrying about entertaining twenty-five guests like last year.

Joe takes his yellow VW. He loves his bug with its funny curved lines and the put-put-put of its spunky motor, but Claire hates it because it has a stick shift, which she doesn't know how to use and refuses to learn because she thinks a stick shift is old-fashioned, and, besides, she always adds, it's a *German* car. She's pressing him to sell it and get a Chevette, instead. He doesn't want a Chevette; he thinks they're ugly, but in the end he knows Claire will probably win this argument, although he's determined to hold on to his VW bug as long as he can.

He's glad he's checking in on Rob. He's worried about his brother. Who wouldn't take the potential ending of a marriage hard, he thinks, as he turns the corner onto Pine Street, but his brother has always taken things especially hard. *Sensitive*, his mother said more than once, always with a tinge of disdain. Sensitive was the opposite of Mom, who had shrugged off setbacks like an alcoholic husband and no money as casually as slipping off a sweater, and glided through the Depression on her looks and charm. As for himself, Claire said he was buoyant, which he didn't quite understand because he didn't consider himself to be outgoing.

"Not outgoing, Joe, *buoyant*," Claire had told him. "You don't let things pull you down."

Doesn't he? That marathon commute is getting him down, draining him day by day, making him grumpy. But maybe Claire is right. He's always tried to look on the bright side of things. During the Depression, when they were living with Grandma Ames, Rob fretted about having to move in with relatives, but Joe, on the other hand, was relieved they had a roof over their head and regular meals.

He's having a hard time being buoyant about his current situation. The layoff, the months of searching, and now the long drive to work every morning. It's wearing on him, the grueling drive, the lack of time with Claire and the girls. But he is forty-six years old and engineers are a dime a dozen these days, and he should be—and he is—grateful to have a job.

He pulls up in front of Rob's house. Before he gets out of the car, he gazes at Lake Michigan for moment. The sparkling blue water never fails to calm him. *This* is why he and Claire live here, in a house that's too small, instead of in a spacious split-level in one of those subdivisions by the expressway sprouting up like dandelions.

He eases out of the VW and sees his brother sitting on the porch swing reading the paper. He's dressed in blue madras plaid shorts and a white polo shirt, and he's shaved for the first time in weeks.

Rob sets down his paper and smiles "Joe! Good to see you."

"I'm running some errands for Claire," Joe says. He eyes his brother. "Looking spiffy, Rob."

"I'm going to a brunch," he says awkwardly. "At Lisa Anderson's. She's a social studies teacher. She lives around the corner."

He exhales and looks sideways at his brother as though daring him to say anything.

Joe cocks an eyebrow.

"Don't give me that look, brother. The invitation was for Amy *and* me," Rob says. "Lisa said you and Claire were welcome, too."

Joe shakes his head. "Claire's going to her ladies' book and art club thing and then we both have things to do to get ready for tonight."

"How about just for a little while, then?"

Joe hesitates. Claire would want him home soon, but she also would want him to encourage Rob to get out and do something other than mope around the house and drink too many gin and tonics. Maybe this brunch will be good for Rob.

"Okay. I'll just stay a few minutes. I'll call Claire and let her know."

Rob nods. "I'll make us some coffee and then we can head over there."

"Good for you, Rob," Joe says. "Let's go."

Chapter 10
Skylar
11:15 a.m.

Today, Zack, Billy, Skye, and Jenny are filming the scene where Benjamin Franklin, John Adams, and Thomas Jefferson are reading Jefferson's draft of the Declaration of Independence and making changes, which Jefferson doesn't like.

They are in the study at Billy's house. He lives in a two-story brick house a few blocks from Skye that Billy says is colonial style. *Expensive* is what Dad said when he dropped her off at Billy's house two weeks ago for their first rehearsal.

Billy's dad is a lawyer, and his home office has a rolltop cherrywood desk and two cherrywood chairs with curved, slatted backs, and a thick floral-patterned wool rug covering the polished hardwood floor. Billy hid the telephone under the desk and put his dad's typewriter and brass desk lamp in the closet, so the room doesn't look modern. His dad is at work—"he's *always* working," Billy told her once—and his mom and sister are at the country club, so they don't have to worry about any adults yelling at them for moving around the furniture.

Billy, who is short and pudgy, and who reminds Skye of Mr. Toad in *Thumbelina*, is John Adams. Skye is Thomas Jefferson. Jenny said Skye *had* to be Thomas Jefferson because she's tall and doesn't have boobs yet. Skye felt a little hurt and kind of mad too when Jenny told her that because she's been wearing a 28A junior bra for almost a year. Jenny said that was no big deal, though, because *she* wears a 32C.

Zack is Benjamin Franklin. Zack is wiry, but he's stuffed a pillow under his shirt to look fat. He's wearing a wig that Billy's mom, who volunteers with the local theater group, gave them to use. A pair of Billy's mom's wire-rim reading glasses are propped on his nose. He's a cute Benjamin Franklin, Skye thinks.

Jenny is playing the chambermaid. Billy had told her when they started working on their movie that she had to play Robert Livingston, the fourth guy who helped write the Declaration of Independence, but Jenny said no way, she'd rather play the serving wench, who at least was doing something useful, than some dude no one ever heard of.

"But that's the point!" Billy had said, "so people learn stuff about history they didn't know. We're doing this for history class, for crying out loud. You think Mrs. Schauser's not going to notice we cut Livingston out? Geez, Jenny, sometimes I can't believe you're in honors history class."

"And we don't even know if there was a serving wench!" Billy had added.

But Jenny had giggled and tossed her hair, and won the argument, and so she's the wench. Skye thinks that Jenny wanted to be the maid just so she can wear a low-cut peasant blouse that shows off her cleavage when she leans over to dust the table. Because she only has a few scenes, Billy has also put Jenny in charge of pressing the play button on the movie camera.

"Okay, Skye, you show me and Zack what you've written. I'll grab the quill pen and start scratching things out, and Zack, nod like you're wise," Billy says. "Jenny, press play and just hold it, okay?'

Zack closes his eyes and says, "I am wise, oh, I am so wise when I'm not screwing women." He opens his eyes and grins.

"Cut it out, Zack," Billy snaps.

Zack shrugs. "It's true. The dude was a tomcat."

Jenny giggles.

"Jenny, just press the play button, okay?" Billy runs his fingers through his bright red hair, which sticks up and makes him look like a mad scientist John Adams.

Jenny sighs and rolls her eyes. Skye feels a little sorry for Billy. He can be kind of a pain in the butt because he bosses them around. But he thought of the idea for their class project, it's his parents' house, and it's his dad's Kodak Instamatic movie camera, so Skye figures he can be bossy if he wants to.

She tugs at the purple velvet pants she's wearing. Billy's mom donated his dad's old leisure suit, and Mom cut the pants off at the knee and hemmed them to look like breeches (Billy's mom called his dad's leisure suit "an unfortunate style error"). Skye's wearing a pair of Dad's black socks, Mom's black loafers, and a white ruffled shirt that Billy's older brother wore to the prom. Her hair is tied back in a ponytail with a black ribbon.

Billy claps his hands. "Okay, guys, places, please!"

"Geez, Billy, you're not Frances Ford Coppola," Zack says. "This isn't *The Godfather*."

Billy flips him off. "You want to direct? Huh, Zack?"

Zack grins at him, shrugs, and clasps his hands together and rests his chin on his hands. "I am so wise," he says. "I am *so* wise. A penny saved is a penny earned."

Billy rubs his hand across his eyes. "Guys, pay attention, okay?"

It's hot in the study because Billy insisted on switching off the air conditioning to make it seem more realistic. He's sweaty and his round face is flushed.

"Zack, stop goofing off. Hold the Declaration and look at it and make marks with your quill pen. Skye, stop staring at Zack."

Skye feels herself blush. Jenny snorts and rolls her eyes again.

"Okay guys! Ready to roll! Jenny, geez, pay attention! Focus for once."

Skye wrinkles her brow and rests her chin on her hand like she's deep in thought. Billy paces back and forth, hands behind his back.

"Action!" he yells. Jenny giggles and presses the button on the movie camera.

"Mr. Jefferson," Billy says. "Have you considered replacing 'God-given right' with 'inalienable rights.'"

Skye frowns like she's insulted by the suggestion.

"Yes, very good, Mr. Adams," Zack says in a deep voice. He picks up the quill pen and pretends to scratch out a couple of words and scribble something on the paper with a flourish.

Skye tries to look dignified as she sits in the straight-backed chair in the corner. She's really admiring Zack's hands. He has beautiful hands with long, thin fingers. He plays saxophone and guitar in the school jazz band. She wonders what it would feel like if he ran his fingers up and down her back.

She hasn't told anyone, not even Jenny, about her crush on Zack, but if she did, she would say that she likes him not only because he is cute with curly hair and pale green eyes, but because he doesn't care what anyone thinks and does what he wants. He's not afraid of any of the teachers, not even crabby old Mrs. Schauser. Last year on April Fools' Day he brought his saxophone into accelerated English class and persuaded everyone to jump on top of their desks and start dancing when Mr. Logano walked in the room. Zack's on the gymnastics team, he gets invited to all the cool parties, and he breezes through his tests and gets straight As, even though he says he doesn't study. He doesn't care about the rumors about his dad, either. Zack says his dad was a college professor from Brazil who was killed in a car accident when he was a baby, but Billy told Skye that he heard his mom and her friends talking at the country club that Zack's mom got knocked up by some anti-war radical guy who wasn't even a student, or maybe it was a janitor who was drafted and went to Vietnam. Skye doesn't believe any of those stories, and even if one of them was true, it doesn't mean anything. Zack is wonderful for who he is, not who his dad was. She had asked Mom about it, and she had pressed her lips together like she does when she's upset and said that gossip wasn't nice and changed the subject.

"Action!" Billy cries. Jenny presses the button on the movie camera. Then she heads toward the kitchen and comes back in carrying a wooden tray with three stainless steel beer steins. The steins are inscribed with the words Middleport Country Club Men's Golf Outing, but Billy told her to place the steins on the tray so the inscriptions face the back. Billy also told her to fill the steins with water for authenticity so they will really be drinking something.

Billy picks up a stein, takes a sip, and splutters.

"Geez, Jenny, that's real beer!"

"I'm in," Zack says and grabs a stein and takes a gulp.

Jenny giggles. "I grabbed it from the fridge."

Billy shakes his head and stomps back to the camera and turns it off. He turns to Jenny. "Yeah, what if my mom counts the cans. Huh?"

Jenny shrugs. "Like your parents are going to care."

Billy glares at her. "My ass would be in trouble if they found out."

Skye thinks Billy has a point. Even though Billy can be a pain in the butt, it *is* his house, or, that is, his parents' house, and Skye doesn't want him to get into trouble.

"It's Billy's house, Jenny," Skye says. Her voice is shaking, but she wants to stick up for Billy. "We could get in a lot of trouble for drinking."

Jenny pouts. "You guys are no fun."

Billy picks up the steins and walks into the kitchen. Skye follows him. He dumps the beer down the sink, fills the mugs with water, and washes them. Skye grabs a dish towel and helps him rinse and dry the mugs.

"Thanks, Skye," Billy mutters. He flips open the garbage can lid and fishes out four empty beer cans.

"Geez, my dad's Coors, too! He brought those all the way back from Colorado last winter when we went skiing at Vail. He guards them like gold," Billy says.

He opens the cabinet beneath the sink, grabs a plastic trash bag, and stuffs the cans inside. "I'll dump these in the trash can by the beach. Dad keeps his extra Coors in the basement fridge." He thinks for a moment, furrowing his forehead. "If I bring a couple up and rearrange the cans in the basement, maybe he won't notice any are missing. I hope."

"Why does he like Coors?" Skye asks.

Bill shrugs. "Because he can't get it here. We all want what we can't have, right?"

Billy opens a cabinet door and places the steins one by one back on the shelf.

"Hey, Skye," He looks back at her. "You're the only one who's helping me here. Thanks."

She shrugs. "Sure."

He stares at her for a moment.

"Look, I know you like Zack. He's a cool guy, but, you know, he has kind of big head. He thinks he's hot stuff."

"He doesn't!" She glances back at the kitchen door and lowers her voice. "You're jealous because he's fun and popular."

Billy is quiet for a moment, considering what she said. Then he shrugs.

"Maybe. Maybe I am."

"And I think you're jealous because Zack's flirting with Jenny," he adds quietly.

Skye feels her face get warm and turns away so Billy can't see her face. She hates that she blushes every time she gets upset.

"I don't know what you're talking about," she says.

They are silent for a moment, then Billy says, "Okay, fine. Listen, we've gotta get back to work. We've only got two more weeks."

As they march back into the study, Skye sees Zack leaning over Jenny, whispering something to her. Jenny smiles and tosses her hair. She got it cut last week in a feathered style, which Jenny said she makes her look older and sophisticated, but Skye thinks it makes her look like an Afghan Hound, which she knows is mean to think, but maybe Billy's right and she's just jealous because Zack is talking to Jenny.

Billy clears his throat.

"Okay, guys, let's do this one more time. Let's finish the scene. Maybe you don't care if you pass honors American history, but *I* do."

Skye settles back into her chair and crosses her arms and tries to look like she's deeply contemplating the Declaration of Independence. Zack looks at her and winks.

She smiles at him, then as Billy glances at her, she quickly resumes her serious Jefferson pose.

She doesn't care what Billy says. Zack is confident, but he's not stuck up and maybe, just maybe, he does like her.

Maybe she might be kissed tonight after all.

"We'll stay for maybe a half hour," Rob says.

They're standing on the porch of Lisa's bungalow. A rocking chair with a blue cushion is on the left side of the porch next to a white wicker table. The porch railing is decorated with red, white, and blue bunting, and a flag-themed wreath hangs on the wooden door, which is painted red and left open to the screen door. Rob hears faint laughter and mellow rock music wafting from the backyard. He's grateful that his brother is with him. He had always socialized with Amy, and going to an event without her feels disconcerting, like being in the rain without an umbrella.

He rings the doorbell. After a moment, he hears footsteps and sees Ted, the high school art teacher, striding through the living room.

"Rob! Good to see you!" Ted says in a smooth voice that reminds him of Richard Burton. "Come on in!"

He opens the door and glances from Rob to Joe.

"This is my brother, Joe," Rob says.

Ted shakes Joe's hand. "Nice to meet you! Party's out back. Lisa's busy with the guests, so I'm helping by letting people in. C'mon."

Ted is tall and lean with shaggy dark hair going gray at his longish sideburns. During the school year he's immaculately turned out in dress pants and tweed blazers, but today he's wearing white flared jeans, a red linen shirt worn untucked, and leather sandals. Harriet has mentioned more than once in the teachers' break room, when Ted isn't there, that Ted is a confirmed bachelor, *if you know what I mean*, with arched eyebrows, and yes, Rob does know what she means, but he doesn't think it's anyone's damn business and ignores the vicious chatter. Ted is a good teacher who keeps his cool even when he's supervising a lunchroom full of rowdy teenagers, and Rob isn't concerned with what he does or who he sees outside of school.

Ted leads them past the living room and down the hallway through a sunny kitchen. Rob gets a fleeting impression of light-colored wood furniture, colorful paintings, shelves crammed with books, a fern in a blue ceramic pot.

The tiny yard is enclosed by a white picket fence. A gravel path winds through small patches of clipped grass lined with terra cotta planters bursting with red and pink geraniums. Clusters of people are talking and laughing, holding drinks, and balancing plates heaped with food. He recognizes a few teachers from school. Rob feels something cold and wet poke at his leg and looks down to see Geo looking up at him, tail wagging. He reaches down and pets the terrier, who grunts in satisfaction and then darts off to snatch a fallen potato chip.

"This is my friend, Martin," says Ted, gesturing to a tall, slender man with curly brown hair and a bushy mustache who has come over to stand by Ted. "We met in grad school," he adds.

Martin holds out his hand. "Nice to meet you, Rob and Joe" he says.

Martin is wearing blue slacks and a blue and red striped button-down shirt. Rob suddenly feels sloppy standing next to Ted and Martin. They both look like they stepped out of a magazine advertisement for a men's clothing store. Rob has never thought much about his appearance. A shirt is a shirt as far as he's concerned, but he's acutely aware at this moment of his wrinkled shorts, the curling collar on his faded polo shirt, and his gut hanging over his belt. He sucks in his stomach. He's gotten scruffy, he realizes, without Amy there to iron his shirts and remind him to take a walk.

"Rob! You came!" Lisa calls, waving to him. She breaks away from the knot of people and heads toward him. She's changed into a short denim skirt and a billowy white off-the-shoulder blouse, and her hair flows in loose waves around her shoulders. She looks relaxed and happy among her throng of friends. *Like a rose in a garden*, he thinks, and then, *Geez, get a grip, I'm still married.*

"Welcome!" she says, smiling. She picks up two Bloody Marys garnished with celery sticks from the table and hands one to Joe and another to Rob. "Happy almost Fourth!"

She touches Rob's shoulder. "Come on, I'll introduce you to people."

He sips his Bloody Mary and follows Lisa. She gestures to a woman with short dark hair and a perky upturned nose. She's standing next to a stocky bearded man wearing a red and white Hawaiian shirt.

"Rob, this is my cousin Linda and her husband, Don."

Don nods and grunts hello as he bites into a chocolate doughnut.

"Nice to meet you," says Linda, holding out her hand. With her pixie haircut and heart-shaped face, she reminds Rob of Claudette Colbert in *It Happened One Night*. Linda has a firm grip, and Rob notices her nails, which are painted red and dusted with blue and silver glitter.

"We work at the same high school, and Rob and his wife live around the corner," Lisa says. Linda raises her eyebrows at the word "wife." Rob realizes that she may have assumed that he was there as Lisa's—what—a date? Special friend? What word was used today, anyway? He feels like he needs to clear up the misconception.

"My wife is up north. Her father's ill," he explains.

"Oh!" Linda says, flustered. She regains her composure. "I—never mind. I'm sorry to hear that."

"He needs help. He has heart failure. It's temporary." *No, it's not*, he thinks, but he's not going to discuss his marital problems here.

"We're trying to get my father to move into a retirement home, but he won't budge," Don says, wiping his hands on a napkin. He picks up another doughnut and takes a bite. "God, these are fantastic. Love the Danish bakeries here."

"Neither will my wife's mother," Joe chimes in, and the four of them dive into a discussion of aging parents. Linda says her mother refuses to use her walker, and Don adds between bites that his father really shouldn't be driving. As they talk, Rob thinks once again that they were lucky that Mom met Chester. Despite the initial awkwardness of their divorced, fun-loving mother marrying Claire's shy, bookish Uncle Chester, making his mother also, he supposes, his aunt by marriage, which is strange when he thinks about it, which he tries not to do. Life would be more complicated now if he and Joe were caring for Mom without patient Chester on the scene.

Rob excuses himself and wanders over to the table to refill his plate. He grabs two deviled eggs and another chocolate doughnut, thinks guiltily that he probably should take up jogging like Joe, and adds a handful of carrots and celery to his plate to balance out the sweet pastry. He glances at his watch and discovers, to his surprise, that almost two hours have gone by and he is enjoying himself.

As much as he would like to stay at this pleasant gathering for a while, he's feeling a bit of a buzz from the two Bloody Marys and he knows Joe needs to get back home.

Joe is in the corner of the yard, talking with a guy with a beard and a flowered red shirt. The man takes his wallet from his back pocket, opens it, and hands a card to Joe, who looks at it, nods, smiles, shakes the man's hand. Joe spots Rob, nods good-bye to the man, and heads over to Joe.

"Who was that?"

"Lisa's cousin's husband. He works at Echo Electronics. He gave me his business card. The company is hiring engineers, and he's going to drop off my resume with the HR lady."

"That's great news!"

Joe shrugs. "Don't want to get my hopes up, but it's a lead. I'll send my resume on Monday."

"Looks like you were having a nice time," Joe adds. "It did you good to get out."

Rob nods. "Actually, I did enjoy myself."

Joe looks at his watch. "Oh, geez. Two already! Claire's going to kill me. I better get back."

Chapter 12
Claire
Noon

Art and Book Club is meeting at Betty' house this month. Betty and Ed live in a white colonial with a screened-in porch opening to a patio with a view of Lake Michigan. Betty has said that the house is too large for them now that their son and oldest daughter are in college and their youngest will graduate from high school next year, but they love the location, and, as Betty said, "eventually, there will be grandkids and we'll need the room."

They're sitting in the screened-in porch, shielded from the sun and mosquitoes, comfortably ensconced in oversized wicker chairs with cabbage rose chintz cushions. On a teakwood coffee table rests the purple vase that Alma created in her pottery class last week, along with an almost-empty glass pitcher of screwdrivers and three glasses on a tray. They enjoy a screwdriver at every month's meeting and this month, in honor of the holiday, Betty is using freshly squeezed orange juice and Ed's special Smirnoff vodka.

Betty, Alma, and Claire decided to still meet this month, even though only three out of their group of seven could attend: Louise and her husband are at their cottage in Minocqua, Doris and her husband and kids are on a camping trip, and Nan and Joan begged off because they are both hosting big Bicentennial bashes and have too much to do. But Betty said that the three of them should still meet.

Betty had said last week, "We need this time for ourselves, ladies! We can't let our little club fall apart because we feel guilty about taking time for ourselves. After all, we have our own identity as women that comes before being a wife or mother. My goodness, our mothers kept the country running during WWII and then the men pushed them right back into the kitchen! We need to nurture our identity as women in our own right!"

Betty joined a women's consciousness-raising group after Ed's "little escapade," as she calls his affair, and since then her conversation has been peppered with phrases like "pass the Equal Rights Amendment" and "consciousness-raising."

It feels daring to be doing this, Claire thinks, taking an hour out of their busy Saturday to discuss a book, when they all have so much to do. Betty is hosting a family gathering tomorrow, Alma is a volunteer parade marshal, and Claire, of course, is entertaining her family for the fireworks tonight.

"It's like skinny dipping in the lake, getting together like this," Alma had commented earlier.

"Working up the courage to do it is the hard part, but then it's so wonderful you wonder why you didn't do it before."

Betty started the club two years ago. Before Ed's affair, Claire never would have dreamed that Betty, the most traditional of all of them—president of the PTA, Girl Scout leader, three children, a leader in the Republican Women, and proud of the "Nixon-Agnew" sign on her front lawn four years ago—would start a women-only book and art club.

Yet Betty had said to her two summers ago, "Let's form an art and book club. Come to my house at 11 a.m. on Saturday."

Betty has a way of saying things like she is giving orders, but it sounded intriguing, and so Claire accepted.

They meet on the first Saturday of every month to discuss a book they have all read, and share something they are working on creatively, whether it's Claire's watercolor painting, Alma's pottery, or Betty's poetry. Betty's husband called it the Old Hens Club, which Claire thinks is rude. Joe calls it her "lady art thing" and in turn, Claire calls his golf league his "guys' golf thing."

Before they begin their discussion of this month's book, *The Bastard* by John Jakes—the first novel in the American Bicentennial series about a family during the American Revolution and the years afterward—

Claire tells them the story of Joe refusing to wash the casserole dish last Wednesday.

"I asked him because I had to take Skye to the mall, but he said he was too tired," Claire says. "He said he drove so far to work five days a week, and he didn't have the energy to wash the dish. It was *one* dish that was soaking in the sink, and I asked him to wash and dry it. He said no. No!"

"And?" Betty asks.

"I said I knew he was tired, but I was tired, too! Then I said I wasn't going to wash it, and I left for the mall with Skye to shop for jeans for her. I was furious at him!"

Betty snorts. "I'd let the dish sit in the sink growing mold until he washed it. I know he has a long drive to work but that doesn't excuse everything."

"It was so unlike him. He's usually so good about helping," Claire says, not wanting to sound like she's being disloyal to Joe.

"I'd consider the circumstances with the drive and all," Alma says. "Cut him some slack."

Alma's husband is a police officer, and she is a guidance counselor. Claire has met Stuart a few times, and he always says, "Be safe out there." She senses Stuart has a dim view of humanity, while Alma, on the other hand, is all about "let's try to understand," and "view the situation from the other person's perspective."

Claire sighs. "I couldn't stand it and got up at 1 a.m. to wash it, and then Joe woke up and finished it, and I felt bad that he missed his sleep on a work night. He gets up at five."

"No guilt!" Betty wags her finger at her. "*No guilt.*"

Betty, Claire thinks, would have terrified even General Patton.

From there they moved on to discuss *The Bastard*. Reading the book caused a bit of controversy. Nan, who isn't even here today, had suggested the book last month as this month's choice, but Betty had balked, saying it wasn't a literary book. Then Alma had retorted that there was no rule that they had to stick to books by dead authors with prose so dense it was like hacking your way through weeds, and after some lively back and forth, Betty had agreed to put it on the schedule in honor of the Bicentennial.

Betty thought it was disappointing.

"Even a fictionalized version of our history should be uplifting and dignified," Betty says. "The novel had so much violence and sex in it."

"But don't you think the inclusion of, er, intimate scenes made it more accessible and modern?" Claire asks. Despite the silly sex scenes and too many fight scenes for her taste, she had enjoyed the novel and had learned so much about the country's history.

"To teenaged boys, maybe," Alma retorts. "My goodness, those descriptions of bosoms spilling out of corsets and . . ."

"Bulges in pants!" Betty says. The women laugh heartily.

"I enjoyed the detailed descriptions of Boston in the 1770s," Claire adds. "The book was well researched."

"It was," Betty agrees. "I'll give Jakes credit for that."

"But the conflict with his mother was too much," Alma says. "It was over the top. But the author is a man, so what can you expect? The mother is always blamed."

"Men and their mother issues!" Betty says. "Damned if you love them, and damned if you don't."

"I'd like to read a book written by a woman with her perspective on history," Alma comments. "It would be a completely different story than the one the men tell."

"Well, you should write one then," Betty says.

Alma snorts. "I don't think anyone would be interested in a book about American history written by a Black woman."

"I'd read it," Claire says. "We need more women writing about history. *Our* stories, not men's stories."

Alma considers this.

"Well, I suppose anything's possible," Alma says. "Maybe I will after I'm retired."

She sets her glass on the tray and picks up her red purse. "Ladies, it's been lovely as always, but I need to get on with my errands. Busy day tomorrow!"

Alma pats her hair self-consciously. At last month's meeting she had declared she was tired of straightening and fussing with her hair, and today she had turned up with her hair in a short, clipped style that Claire thinks looks stylish and cool for summer.

"Still getting used to my short hair," Alma murmurs. "I don't think Stu likes it."

"Tell him he needs to change with the times!" Betty booms. "It's not the 1950s. It's the 1970s, and we women are liberated!"

"Yes, indeed," says Alma. "Times are changing! Stu will just have to get used to it."

"Before you go, a last toast." Betty holds up her glass, which holds her nearly finished second screwdriver, and Alma and Claire lift their empty glasses with the bits of melting ice left from their first and only drink.

"Ladies, here's to our Bicentennial," Betty says. She takes a hearty sip. "Now, back to our battle stations."

"To the Bicentennial," Alma, Claire, and Betty say in unison.

Then they help Betty carry the glasses and tray back into the kitchen, say goodbye, and get on with their day.

Claire had ridden her bike to Betty's house, and she decides to bike downtown to pick up paper cups and napkins at Dillworth's Five and Dime. She had asked Joe to stop, but Joe wasn't home yet from that brunch by the time she left for Art and Book Club. In any case, he might forget and, if not, she can save the extra cups and napkins for next year.

She is glad Joe stopped by to see Rob. They are both worried about Rob, moping about Amy, drinking too many gin and tonics, and watching soap operas every afternoon. She's pleased that Rob was interested in finally getting out and doing something, and Joe was there to keep an eye on him.

The problem, Claire thinks as she pedals her trusty blue Schwinn down Elm Street and turns on to Main, puffing a bit—she really needs to start walking more—is that Rob is a rescuer, and he can't save Amy from her unhappiness. Claire muses that Rob is different from Joe, who isn't a rescuer or rescuee (is that even a word? She'll have to look it up), but more like a happy survivor with the remarkable ability to toss off setbacks like Honey shaking herself off after a bath. She'd seen it all those years ago, when he was a fifteen-year-old making deliveries for the pharmacy. Joe's father was beaten down from working at the gas station, and the family had bounced around from one rundown apartment to another until they finally moved in with their grandmother, yet Joe always had a smile and a cheerful hello, and he was willing to ride his bike to make deliveries no matter if it was raining or bitterly cold.

"Hard worker, that Joe," her father would say. "He's not going to be a delivery boy the rest of his life."

She wonders if the same pattern is repeating itself in her girls. Grace was like Joe; she'd adapt and float back to the top no matter what happened between her and Ben—break up with him, drop the trip to France, stay with him—she'd be fine. Grace, like herself, has a practical streak. Skye, though—well, she is more like Rob, Claire muses. That boy, Zack, that Skye is always talking about, "Zack said this, Zack was so funny." It's obvious Skye is crazy about him in a junior high school crush way, but Claire worries that her daughter will get her heart broken. She's met Zack a few times when she's dropped Skye off for rehearsals for their summer school project. He's polite, but politeness isn't the same thing as kindness and sincerity. He's a little too full of himself, in Claire's opinion, and too restless, although she wonders if that's a cover-up for the anxiety he may feel about that whole mystery of his father. She remembers Betty gossiping about that years ago before she believed in women's consciousness-raising and solidarity and still liked juicy gossip. Zack's mother, Judge Grainger's daughter, going out East to college—what was it, Smith? Bryn Mawr? Columbia?—and coming home pregnant. The mother's version, Betty said, was that Elaine's husband was a professor who was killed in a car crash, but Betty said that they weren't married and he wasn't even a student, much less a professor. But whatever the truth, Elaine moved back home, earned her nursing degree, and is now head nurse in obstetrics at Middleport Hospital. Good for her, Claire thinks. She may spoil her son, but she made a life for herself, and whether she was married when she had Zachary is her own business.

But Skye, unlike Grace, takes everything to heart. Sensitive, like Rob, and Mike for that matter, who could be prone to bouts of melancholy for all his gregariousness. Claire turns on to Main Street. The street is busy, so she hops off her bike and walks it on the sidewalk, searching for a lamppost or parking meter to lock her bike. Skye needs a new hobby or club, Claire decides, to meet new friends. Would she like tennis lessons, perhaps? Or something artistic, like painting? She adds *find something for Skye to do this summer* to her list of issues to worry about.

As she passes the boarded-up stores, she feels a pinch of sadness. When she was a girl, downtown was the place to be on a Saturday night. But Zimmer's Department Store went out of business last year, the candy shop is gone, the butcher shop closed years ago, and her father's drugstore is boarded up and empty because the pharmacist who bought it after her father died sold the building five years ago and moved his business to the mall. She looks quickly away from the vacant building. So many memories . . . sitting at the lunch counter after school, talking with the cute young delivery boy who became her husband . . . She shakes her head. No use dwelling on the past glory days of downtown. No one wanted to shop downtown anymore. It was too old and worn down and too far from the new subdivisions.

She locks her bike around a light pole and heads toward Dillworth's. As she walks past the old Neapolitan movie theater, she feels another twinge of sadness. It used to be such a beautiful theater with its plush red velvet seats and a domed ceiling painted with gold and silver stars. She saw so many wonderful movies there—*The Wizard of Oz, Mrs. Miniver, Bells of St. Mary's, Laura* . . . and now the front doors are grimy, one window is broken and covered with plywood, and the dirty, glass-encased poster next to the shuttered ticket booth says *XXX-rated*!

Dillworth's is two doors past the Neapolitan. Despite the empty building surrounding it, the five-and-dime has held on because the merchandise is cheap and the store stocks items that people always need, like aspirin, paper clips, and birthday cards. Claire pushes through the revolving glass door and heads toward the paper goods aisle. She picks out paper plates printed with red, white, and blue stars, and paper cups that say *1776–1976* and joins the end of a long line of customers holding boxes of sparklers, packages of napkins, cases of soda, and bags of chips.

She winces as she sees who the cashier is today. It's Marcie Peterson, who married Claire's old high school crush, Mason. He was the captain of the football team and had asked Claire to the homecoming dance in her junior year, but he had jilted her a week later by telling her that she was a swell girl, but he thought of her like a kid sister. Her heart was broken when he took Marcie to the dance instead. At the time Marcie was a vivacious cheerleader with curly hair and dimples. But, Claire thought, she was really very lucky that Mason dumped her because she started dating Joe a year later, and despite their fights over silly things like the casserole dish, he truly was a keeper. She had heard that Mason married Marcie, got a job in the auto factory, gained weight, drank too much beer, and died in a car crash on his way home from a bar three years ago, and now Marcie was making extra money working at Dillworth's on the weekends.

"Hello, Claire," Marcie says as she rings up the napkins and cups. She looks tired and older than forty-five, Claire thinks, with dark circles under her eyes and her graying brown hair cut in a choppy shag. While shag cuts are fashionable, Claire thinks the style makes women look tough, and she clings to her smooth chin-length bob, old-fashioned though it may be.

"Hello, Marcie," Claire says. "Happy Fourth."

Marcie nods. "And you, Claire. Happy Fourth."

Claire hands her money to Marcie, and exits the dime store, relieved that the long line behind her meant that she didn't need to linger for small talk with Marcie. Even though she is grateful that things turned out the way they did, and she feels sorry for Marcie now, but seeing her still brings back that pang, silly as it is all these years later, of seeing Mason and Marcie dancing in the high school gym. That's why she's worried about Skye and Grace. She knows that the fallout from those first crushes and loves can linger for years. Vivian, for instance, never married, and while she insists that she's too independent to ever marry, Claire suspects her sister may never have quite gotten over breaking things off with Greg. Vivian mentioned on the phone a few weeks ago that Greg had moved back to Wisconsin and they had met for lunch, but Vivian has said nothing about it since then, and Claire fears that their reunion did not go well.

On her way back to her bike, she stops in front of Romero's Resale Store. A closed sign hangs across the grimy front door. She had heard the store had closed last month. She peers through the dirt-streaked window. Inside, a row of washing machines lines the wall, bulky old radios are stacked haphazardly on a shelf, and vacuums are jammed in the back. As Claire looks at the dim, cluttered interior, she thinks back to when the building was Svenson's Scandinavian Home Goods. She remembers when it was a sunny, airy store with thick blue rugs covering a polished parquet floor, and pale-yellow walls edged with creamy crown molding. Mom would take her and Vivian there a few times a year as a treat. They'd admire the porcelain plates decorated with delicate flowers, the glass vases, the soft linen napkins, and lacy table runners. The store had a tiny café in the raised alcove in the back, and they'd eat open-faced tuna and egg salad sandwiches on rye bread, and for dessert they would each order a dish of vanilla ice cream drizzled with caramel sauce and slivered almonds and served in a silver bowl.

She's lost in thought, thinking of those long-ago lunches, when the door opens. A heavyset man about forty with thinning dark hair and a sweaty face pokes his head out.

"Can I help you?"

She jumps back, startled. "I'm sorry, I thought the store was closed."

"It is. I was in the basement trying to make sense of things. I just popped up for lunch." He steps outside and holds out his hand. "Gil Romero. Pop owned this place."

Claire nods. "I read in the paper that it closed."

"Yep. Dad had a heart attack—he's fine, but it was a scare—and he decided he was done, closed the shop, and moved to Florida with his lady friend."

He shook his head and smiled wryly. "And left *me* to figure out what to do with the building."

She had heard Romero was an ornery man, eccentric, but shrewd, with a reputation for selling reliable used appliances. His son has a courteous face, she thinks, but he looks frazzled.

He fishes in his pocket and hands her a card. "That's the realtor helping me sell or rent the place. If you know anyone interested, tell them to call. The rent will be dirt cheap. I don't want the building sitting empty, and not many people are interested in starting a business downtown anymore."

"I will," Claire says, slipping the card in her purse. "I remember when this was Svenson's."

Gil nods. "Yep, me too."

"My mother would take my sister and me here for lunch occasionally as a treat. I loved it."

"Hmm." Gil shifts from one foot to the other, then looks at Claire. "My mom was the cleaning lady for Svenson's."

There is an awkward pause between them.

"Oh, I see," Claire says. Claire worries she's put her foot in her mouth, babbling about having lunch at the place where his mother cleaned.

"Your mother did a beautiful job," Claire says quickly. "The store was always spotless and smelled like lemon furniture polish."

He beams and nods. "Mom said it was her favorite place to clean with all that beautiful stuff they had there. The money she earned cleaning buildings got my sister and me through college."

He shakes his head. "She always wanted to travel to Sweden after she retired because of working at Svenson's and seeing all the pretty things imported from there, but she got breast cancer and passed away before she could."

"I am so sorry," Claire says. "My father wanted to travel, too, out West, but he had a heart attack. He owned the drugstore—Jansen's."

Gil smiles. "Oh, yeah, Mom would take me sometimes to get a chocolate malt at the soda counter. Best in town."

"Thank you. My father told the soda jerks to use lots of chocolate malt and ice cream, no skimping."

"You could tell!" Gil adds, "I guess you have to do what you want while you can. I shut down my accounting office every summer for two weeks and my wife and I take the kids on a trip. We went to Williamsburg this year, for the Bicentennial, and we're going to Texas next year. Rita says we should save for a few more years before taking another vacation, but—" he shrugs "—the kids get older and then they don't want to go on vacation with their parents. They'd rather hang out at the mall."

"They don't want to be seen with their parents," Claire agrees. "I think it's smart to go on a vacation with your kids while they still want to go." She thinks about the road trips they took as a family—a two-week trip to Yosemite, a week in Niagara Falls, a trip to Florida, and a week in Washington D.C., plus the yearly trips to a cottage up north—and she wishes they had done more. The girls had grown up so fast. Grace is an adult now and Skye is already a teenager. Maybe they could take Skye somewhere over spring break, or maybe they could go somewhere next summer after Grace returns from France.

"You bet." Gil nods, then turns and locks the door. "I'm off to grab some lunch. If you know anyone who is interested in renting, tell them to give me a call."

"Of course," Claire says. He waves goodbye and Claire turns back to the window. As she looks at the sign that says *Romero's Resale Appliances*, she suddenly sees something different in her mind. She imagines a coffee shop with walls filled with photographs and paintings created by women. She sees colorfully painted wooden tables and chairs, and a comfortable sofa in the alcove. She sees a place where women can write poems, draw in sketchbooks, read books, drink coffee, and talk with one another.

Heart. The name pops into her head. HerArt and a logo of a heart with a . . . maybe a paintbrush beneath it. No. It's crazy, it's impossible . . . and yet, she has a bit of money. If the rent is as cheap as Gil Romero said it would be, her savings would cover the first few months. No, it is impossible. She should use that money for an air conditioner or Skye's college fund or . . . And yet, she does have a small nest egg that Mom gave to her and Vivian after Dad died, from his life insurance money. She and Joe have dipped into it occasionally for house repairs and college costs, but perhaps she could use some of it to get the business started until sales from artwork provide an income.

She pulls out the card, stares at it, and tucks it back into her purse.

Before she heads to the airport, Kitty stops at Oakwood Cemetery. It's on the outskirts of Middleport, surrounded by farmland. She and Frederick had chosen the cemetery, first for Mike, and then for themselves when the time came. Kitty likes that the cemetery is sunny, not gloomy like the two cemeteries in town. It's an expanse of green dotted with small ponds and bordered by oak, birch, and pine trees, peaceful and lovely. Mike played baseball in high school, and he loved nothing more than to be outside on a sunny day. Kitty likes to think that the cemetery would have reminded him of a baseball field.

The cemetery is quiet today. Kitty assumes that most people are busy today with their holiday plans. A few people are scattered about the cemetery—a couple filling a vase with water, a solitary woman clipping grass around a grave marker, and an older man holding a bouquet of flowers leaning over a gravestone.

Carrying a thermos of water and a bouquet of red, white, and blue carnations wrapped in cellophane, she walks the few steps to Mike's grave. She and Frederick had picked a plot by the road so it would be easier for them to visit when they were older. *And now I am older*, she thinks, *thirty-two years have gone by since I first stood at my son's grave.*

She pauses for a moment to look at her husband's gravestone. *Frederick Edward Jansen, Aug. 21, 1900–Nov. 14, 1960.* She presses two fingers to her lips, kisses them, and blows the kiss down to her husband's plot, a little ritual she does every time she visits. Then she turns her attention to her son, *Michael Frederick Jansen, Feb. 12, 1924–June 7, 1944. Beloved son and brother.* For the first few years she sobbed every time she'd read those words, but the years have softened the pain to a gentle ache that washes over her and recedes. She bites her lip, then briskly unscrews the thermos, pours water into each of the iron vases, unwraps the bouquet, and arranges the flowers on both gravestones. She fusses with the carnations, tucking a red one here, a blue one there, and a white one in the middle as a breeze rustles the leaves of nearby oak trees. Robins chirp and frogs croak in the pond. It's peaceful here. A good place for her son and husband to rest.

"Happy Fourth of July, Frederick. Happy Fourth of July, Mike, my son," she whispers, and walks slowly back to her car.

Traffic is heavy as she turns onto Howell Avenue. She had left in plenty of time, though, so she would still arrive two hours before her flight. She turns into the airport and follows the signs to the parking garage. She carefully parks her Oldsmobile and retrieves her suitcase from the trunk. Though she tried to pack light, it's heavy. She had thought about how she was going to carry her bag by herself from the garage to the ticket counter and came up with an idea—after all, she and Agnes are going to have to be as resourceful as two old ladies on a road trip adventure can be! She opens her purse, takes out a pink chiffon scarf, ties one end around the handle and drags her suitcase toward the elevator. It bumps along the ground, but it's much easier to pull than carry.

She checks in at the ticket counter, gratefully hands over her heavy suitcase to the ticket agent, then makes her way through the terminal. What a monstrosity the security gate might be, she thinks, remembering how she and Frederick walked right from the ticket counter onto the plane when they flew to New York. This time she'll pass through a metal detector as she boards. The agent had assured her it was painless.

She buys a Coke and a hotdog from a counter in the terminal and settles on an orange plastic seat by the gate. She pulls the July *Good Housekeeping* from her straw tote bag to read while she waits.

A young couple is sitting across from her, both wearing faded jeans, T-shirts, and thick-soled sandals. Two worn canvas backpacks are set by their feet. Next to them, an older man with thick unruly eyebrows is reading *Jaws*. His eyebrows rise in surprise, and he flips back to re-read a page. She hasn't read the book or seen the movie, but Claire has seen it, and she told Kitty that it made her think twice about even dipping her toe in Lake Michigan, even though there are no sharks in the lake, of course.

Kitty pushes aside the unpleasant thought of sharks and thinks, instead, about the last time she flew on a plane—the third time she ever was on an airplane. Frederick had surprised her with a trip to New York City for their fortieth wedding anniversary. They had stayed at the Plaza, saw *Bye, Bye Birdie* on Broadway, and strolled through Central Park. They bought hot dogs from a street vendor. Kitty still remembers the crisp, savory taste of that hot dog, so different from the lukewarm rubbery one she's nibbling now. She can't finish it, and stands up slowly, mindful of her knees, and tosses the remains of the hot dog in a nearby trash can. She'll be served something on the flight, she assumes, a meal, perhaps, or a snack.

She sits down and returns to her happy memories of their trip to New York. Kitty had loved every moment of the flight, the courteous stewardesses in their crisp uniforms and white gloves, the passengers dressed up for the journey, men in suits, women in dresses and gloves and hats, the lunch served on white china, the soothing drone of the engines. Frederick had hated the flight. He thought it was unnatural to be hurtling through the air in a metal tube. He had, in fact, wanted to take the train or drive to New York, but Kitty had put her foot down. They were *not* driving for two days to New York and two days back or sleeping in a cramped train compartment. No, she had told him they had the money to fly to New York, and they were going to travel by air, and that was that.

They had a marvelous time, and those memories, along with all her other memories, were what got her through those awful months after Frederick died, three months after their trip, dropping dead from a heart attack at the pharmacy counter.

Kitty clenches and unclenches her hand. Frederick has been gone sixteen years, and although her grief has softened, sometimes a memory like this one brings a sharp stab of pain. He was only sixty. So young; he could have lived another twenty years. All those long days in the pharmacy, the half pack of cigarettes he smoked every day, all that worry. All those unrealized plans for what they were going to do after he retired: traveling, spending time with the girls, and vacationing in Hayward in the summer and driving to Florida in the winter.

She glances at the young couple sitting across from her. Their arms are wrapped around each other, and they kiss each other in a way she feels is far too intimate for a public area. The girl's curly dark hair hangs in her eyes, and her boyfriend's shaggy blond hair is almost as long as hers. The girl is wearing a tight black tank top and ripped jeans; the boy's wrinkled gray T-shirt says, "Get Stoned." Stoned? She thinks that means smoking marijuana;t she's not quite sure.

What a difference sixteen years makes, Kitty thinks. She tries to picture the girl across from her in a pastel sheath dress and pink pumps with a matching hat and her hair neatly twisted in a chignon. She tries to imagine her disheveled boyfriend with a crew cut and a navy-blue suit and narrow black tie. But she can't picture it. She simply can't. The world is so different now that she can't overlay the past on the present; it would be like placing a lacy doily over a cigarette burn on a table.

It bewilders her, the young people's pounding music, their insistence on wearing denim everywhere, the dope they smoke, and the way young men and women live together and don't care who knows it. It's not that living together like that is exactly shocking to her—after all, her friend Phyllis went to New York after high school to become a dancer—what a scandal that was! And from the letters that Phyllis wrote to her, letters that Kitty never dared to show her mother, all sorts of wild things went on: affairs, speakeasies, cocaine, prostitution. But that was New York in the 1920s, not Kitty's snug little world. She wants to withdraw in her own world now: her memories of Frederick and her children when they were little, her girlhood, her world. But her yearning to simply withdraw into her memories is precisely why she is going on this trip.

"We can be fossils when we're ninety, Kitty!" Agnes had said. "We can't be fossils when we're seventy-four. Let's have an adventure while we still can, see a bit of the world."

She wonders if Claire has stopped at her house yet. Kitty pictures her seeing the letter propped on the table, reading it, and shaking her head at what she would think of as her mother's folly. She pictures Claire calling Joe and saying, "You would not believe what Mom just did!"

Kitty will call Claire and Joe this evening if they don't call her first. Kitty is sure that when she calls Claire, she will give her a list of reminders. *Wear a hat. Don't overexert yourself. Look out for rattlesnakes. Drink plenty of water.*

Kitty doesn't remember ever giving her children a list of instructions every time they left the house. That is, except when Mike left that last time after his leave, and all the good that did for him. *Be careful,* millions of mothers told their sons, as if those words could protect them against bullets and bombs. All those telegrams were handed to mothers and fathers and wives. All those gold stars in windows.

What would Mike say if he were here? She hopes that he would be happy for her. Perhaps he would have said to Claire, *Don't worry about Mom, she's a tough old bird.*

But of course, she doesn't know, has no idea of what her son would have been like or what he would have said at age fifty-two, and that's the heartache that will never go away.

When she talks with Claire and Joe, she will tell them that she will be fine, she's healthy and, in fact, her own mother lived until eighty-nine, sharp as a tack until the end.

But when Kitty thinks of her mother at his moment, she doesn't think of her at eighty-nine, with her thinning gray hair and shriveled skin. No, to her, her mother will be forever thirty-five and beautiful, making hot cocoa for Kitty as she tells her mother about her day at school.

Someday, Mama, Agnes and I are going to visit the Yosemite and Yellowstone!

Well, my darling girl, you better do it before you get married, for after that there will no time to travel.

Now, sixty years after her Girl Scout days, she is finally going to do it. She and Agnes are going to follow through with the plans they had made when they were twelve years old to visit Yellowstone, the national park that Miss Adams had described to them.

She can't wait for her adventure to begin.

After seven takes, they finally finish the scene. Skye and Jenny had planned to go to Big Beach after they were done, but Jenny says it's too hot now to hang out on the beach, and she tells Skye she wants to go home for a while and will meet her tonight at the park. They are going to watch Zack perform with the Middleport Junior High Jazz Band at the Bicentennial Eve concert. Jenny waves good-bye to Skye, hops on her bike, and pedals down the street. Zack says he has to cut the grass for his mom, and he gets on his bike and leaves too. Billy asks her to look at his stamp collection in his bedroom, but there is no way she is going to Billy's bedroom. He reminds her of a frog, a sweet frog, but a frog nonetheless with his round bulging eyes and thick glasses. Grandma Kitty said to her once, "You have to kiss a few frogs before you find your prince," but Skye told her that Billy was a frog she'd rather not kiss.

Skye decides to stop at Grandma Kitty's house to say hello before heading home. She likes to go to Grandma Kitty's house by herself sometimes. It's peaceful there. Grandma Kitty doesn't ask her stupid questions like, *How's school*? She doesn't ask her why she isn't going to the fall dance or suggest that she should clip the hair out of her eyes or wear a skirt instead of jeans. She says, "What's new in your life, Miss Skylar?" and then Skye talks to her grandmother about whatever she feels like, or nothing at all, and Grandma Kitty will tell Skye about her day playing bridge with her friends and share her latest letter from Agnes. Sometimes they don't talk at all and sit in companionable silence at the pink Formica kitchen table as Grandma Kitty does the crossword puzzle in the *Middleport Gazette* and Skye reads a Nancy Drew book and they both nibble on the bowl of chocolate bridge mix from Dillworth's.

Skye goes to the back door, which Grandma Kitty usually keeps open to the screen door in the summer to let in the breeze. The door is shut tightly. Skye tries the handle on the heavy wood door, but it's locked. Skye frowns. It's not Grandma Kitty's shopping and errand day, and it's not her bridge club day, either. Where could she be?

Skye decides to check inside. Sometimes Grandma Kitty takes a nap during the day, and she doesn't mind when Skye lets herself in. Besides, Grandma Kitty has high blood pressure, and Skye has overheard Mom and Dad talking about Grandma Kitty's heart condition, atrial something or other, and maybe Grandma Kitty is sick.

Skye gets Grandma Kitty's spare key from beneath the flowerpot by the garage. She turns the lock and pushes open the door, which squeaks as she opens it.

"Grandma Kitty!" she calls. There is no sound and the air in the kitchen is warm and smells a little musty.

"Grandma Kitty?"

She peers in the living room. No one is there. Skye feels a prickle of anxiety. What if Grandma Kitty fell and broke a hip, something that Mom worries about? What if she fainted? She peeks into Grandma Kitty's bedroom. The bed is neatly made up with the pink damask bedspread and pillows perfectly in place, and the room smells faintly of Coty face power. Grandma Kitty isn't there, either. Skye feels relieved because was nervous she would find Grandma Kitty lying unconscious on the floor.

She guesses she should check the basement next, but before she does, she goes to the kitchen to get a drink of water. She knows she's just stalling because she doesn't want to go in the basement. Even though she's thirteen, the dark basement still scares her a little. As she reaches for a glass in the cupboard, she notices a letter on the kitchen table, propped up against a pink vase filled with silk flowers. The letter is addressed to *Claire*. Mom. Skye hesitates a second and grabs the letter and opens it. She knows it's wrong to read a letter addressed to someone else, but maybe Grandma Kitty went to the hospital or something and wrote this letter while she was gasping for breath. Maybe she tried calling Mom and no one was home. Skye reads the letter, gasps, stuffs the letter into her denim shorts pocket, and dashes outside to the garage. She grabs the metal handle on the wooden garage door and carefully pushes up the door. It's heavy and creaks as she wrestles it up. The garage is empty. Grandma Kitty's blue Oldsmobile is gone.

She suddenly remembers she didn't lock the door, runs back and locks it, puts the key back under the flowerpot, hops on her bike and pedals feverishly toward home.

Rob had a surprisingly nice time at the party. He liked Lisa's friends and enjoyed talking with them. Joe had enjoyed himself, too, and he got the lead for an open position as an engineer. It's after 2 p.m. when he and Joe head back to his house.

Between the two Bloody Marys, the sun and humidity, and, perhaps, the zing of attraction he felt when Lisa had squeezed his hand when they were leaving and said, "Would you like to come along with me on Tuesday when I'm walking Geo?", Rob is feeling lightheaded. He stumbles over a crack in the sidewalk, and Joe grabs his elbow.

"Careful, little brother," Joe says.

Rob grunts. "I'm fine."

"Claire's going to give me an earful for coming back late, but I'm glad we went to the party. It was fun. Lisa is nice."

Rob glances at his brother, whose face has that bland look when he says something to rile him up and pretends it's nothing. "I'm still married, Joe."

"I'm not saying go to bed with her. I'm just saying say hello to Lisa when she's walking her dog. Talk to people. Get out of the house again."

"And you get your resume in the mail on Monday," Rob says to change the subject.

"Will do, Rob. Will do."

They reach Rob's house. Joe gives him an awkward hug.

"Glad you got out, Rob."

"Well, with Amy gone, I . . ."

"But she's not here," Joe says. He looks at his brother.

"I know," Rob says quietly. "I know."

Joe pats his brother's shoulder, nods good-bye. He heads toward his VW parked on the street, turns back to Rob and says, "Eight tonight for the fireworks! Be there!" Joe takes a step, stops, turns back to Rob again, and says, "The cups and napkins! I forgot to go the store, damn it!"

"She probably already got them," Rob calls to his brother.

He waves and watches his long-legged brother fold himself into his VW. Rob imagines Claire will give him an earful for being gone so long and forgetting to stop at the store. Claire is feistier than Amy. He's sleepy from the Bloody Marys, but he doesn't feel like snoozing right now. It seems like a waste of time in the middle of this beautiful day. He realizes this is the first time in weeks that he hasn't felt like a nap on the couch is the best thing to do with his time. He looks at the ragged lawn and overgrown bushes. The house looks sad and uncared for. He doesn't want it to look like that when Sam comes home tomorrow. He heads to the garage. He'll cut the grass now—it's a manual push mower so even in his slightly inebriated state he can't hurt himself—and tackle the bushes tomorrow.

For the first time since Amy left, he realizes with a start, he feels something other than sadness. He feels . . . maybe . . . sort of okay.

It's been a good day, Claire thinks as she slices cucumbers in the kitchen. She enjoyed the book club discussion with Alma and Betty, and ideas for the old Svenson's space are swirling through her mind. Crazy idea, why is she even thinking of it, but still . . . that old junk shop is in horrible shape, true, but the potential . . . She'll have to talk with Joe about it, of course, but wouldn't it be wonderful if she *could* do it? No, it's a silly idea, she should put it out of her mind, and yet . . .

Skye burst through the kitchen door, red-faced and out of breath.

"Mom! Mom! Grandma's going to Denver today!" Skye says, waving an envelope in her face.

"What?" Skye thrusts the envelope in her hand. Claire looks at it, puzzled, and sees her name on the envelope in her mother's neat handwriting. She glances at Skye, takes out a piece of pink stationery paper, and unfolds it.

I'm off on a little trip with Agnes. We're going to explore some of the national parks . . .

Claire scans the letter and looks up at Skye.

"What on earth? Where did you get this? Did Grandma give this to you?"

Skye shakes her head. "No, I stopped at Grandma's house on the way home and she wasn't there. I saw this letter on the kitchen table. I'm sorry I opened it, but I thought maybe she was at the hospital or something."

Claire glances at the letter again. The flight leaves at 3:30. It's after two now. Where is Joe? He should be back by now. She'll give him fifteen minutes, and if he's not home, she'll drive to the airport herself. She's not letting Mom fly off to Denver for God knows what type of adventure without saying good-bye.

Joe had prodded Rob to go out to get him out of the house and stop moping about Amy for a few hours. But he'd enjoyed himself, too. He had thought he'd feel awkward, not knowing anyone, but Lisa's friends were friendly and fun, and he discovered that Lisa's cousin's husband—Don? Yes, that was his name. He works for Echo Electronics, and he had handed Joe his business card, saying he had heard of an opening for a senior engineer, if he was interested. "It's not a managerial job" Don had said almost apologetically, "but send me your resume and I'll bring it to HR."

A job twenty minutes away from home! He would save more than an hour of driving each way, time he could use to sleep later, spend more time with Claire and the girls, and work in the yard. Exercise. Read. It would almost be like being on vacation every day. Of course, he was way ahead of himself. All he had was a business card, and maybe Don would forget they had talked. But it was a start.

He'd send in his resume and his best cover letter— he'd ask Claire to help him with it—and then he could only hope.

He parks the VW in the driveway and as he's getting out the kitchen door flies open, and Claire rushes out, Skye at her heels.

"What took you so long! You said you'd only stay at that brunch a half hour!"

"We got to talking to people and Rob was having a good time, so . . ." He feels his good mood evaporate. He can tell that Claire is in one of her moods, annoyed about something or other.

"Never mind," Claire says. "Come on, we have to get to the airport! Now!"

"What? Why? Airport?" Clearly a lot has happened in the past three hours.

"Grandma is flying to Denver, Dad," Skye pipes up. She's grinning like it's an adventure from one of her books.

"Grandma Kitty? Denver?" He's trying to keep up.

"That's what I said!" Claire snaps. "I'll explain on the way."

Claire opens the passenger door of the VW and hops in. Skye scrambles in the back seat. Claire motions to Joe to get back in the car.

"Get in, Joe! We've got to go!"

Joe sighs and gets in the car. He buckles his seatbelt, shoves the key in the ignition switch, puts his hands on the steering wheel, and turns to his wife.

"Now what did your mother do?"

The Middleport Marina deli and convenience store is busy with boaters stocking up on ice, soda, suntan lotion, and sandwiches. Grace is working at the deli counter with Frannie. She looks like she's eighty with her wiry gray hair and bony, wrinkled, tanned face, but she's only sixty-three. She reminds Grace of a woman in one of those Dorothea Lange photographs of families during the Great Depression that she learned about in history class. That is, if Lange's "Mother of Seven Children" had a perm and wore a Milwaukee Brewers shirt, like Frannie is wearing today. Frannie is a big Milwaukee Brewers fan (even though Grace noticed that she still calls them the Braves half the time, like her parents do), and they are playing the Red Sox tonight, and Frannie said she's going to be listening to the game this evening while drinking a Pabst and doing her ironing.

Frannie told Grace her whole story last summer when they were working at the deli counter together, and she told Grace her whole story again this year as they've sliced deli meat and wrapped sandwiches together. Grace isn't sure if Frannie forgot she told her the story last year or if she just likes to hear herself talk.

Frannie's husband died twenty years ago of a stroke, her daughter, Darla, finally divorced her no-good husband, and now Darla and her daughter are living with Frannie in a two-bedroom apartment. Frannie is eking out a living for the three of them between her pension from working as a cashier in the high school cafeteria and what she earns working in the marina deli in the summer while Darla attends community college to become a licensed practical nurse.

"So, you told him you gotta talk," Frannie says as she slaps mayonnaise on a turkey sandwich. "Bet he's stewing on that."

"He's bothered that I'm leaving," Grace says, as she slides two ham sandwiches into a paper bag and hands it to a balding sunburned man with beery breath. "But it's not fair to him, me going to France for almost a year. It really isn't."

"What about you?" Frannie turns to Grace, hands on hips. "Men are a problem."

She points a plastic-gloved finger at Grace. "Do yourself a favor. Get men out of your life, and you'll be happier."

"I don't know about that," Grace says. Life without men sounds like, well, like living like a nun, and she doesn't want that, but it's too hot and too many people are in line to get into a debate with Frannie right now.

Frannie shakes her head and turns back to assembling turkey sandwiches, yanking the bread from the plastic bag and throwing slices of turkey on top of the bread with what seems to Grace like unnecessary force.

She has to let Ben go, she thinks. It is the right thing to do. It's not fair to him to wait almost a whole year for her to return from France, and it's not fair to her, either, to be tied to someone 4,000 miles away.

But when she thinks of breaking things off with Ben, she feels sad, not relieved or happy. She sees his gentle face with his warm brown eyes looking confused and sad, and she imagines herself regretting the words even as she says them. It's only July. They can enjoy the summer and then she can think about it later, right?

"Grace!" She looks up and sees her friend Heidi pushing her way to the counter. This summer Heidi has moved on from her Stevie Nicks phase to her Carly Simon one; she's stopped bleaching her hair and has swapped her lacy shirts and long skirts for a floppy suede hat, T-shirts, and blue jean shorts.

"Wait your turn, lady!" an older woman says.

"I'm just talking to my friend," Heidi says, sliding past the woman. She stands in front of the counter and holds up two tickets.

"Want to go to the Sullivan Center open house?"

"I'm at work until three . . ."

Heidi places the tickets on the counter and pushes them toward her.

"I got them from work, but I can't go because Hank and I have to go to his aunt's stupid barbecue. But you can go!"

"Ben is working, I don't have anyone to go with."

"Go by yourself. It will be fun! Fancy food, music, and maybe some good-looking men!"

"Yeah, go by yourself. Or bring me!" Frannie says.

"I can't. Ben's working."

Heidi waves her hand dismissively. "He's working all night, so go enjoy yourself."

"Enjoy yourself, Grace!" Frannie says.

"Yeah, enjoy yourself, sweetheart!" chimes in the man with the beery breath.

"Shut up," Frannie says to the man. "Yeah, Grace, go. Enjoy yourself."

Why not? It might be fun. Ben won't mind, she thinks. He'd want her to go and have fun for a few hours.

"Thanks, Heidi. Maybe I will," she says, slipping the ticket in the pocket of her shorts.

"Cool!" Heidi says. "Gotta go to that stupid barbecue now." She elbows her way back through the crowd. She turns and waves at Grace.

"See you tomorrow at the beach!"

"Hey, lady, I'm waiting for my sandwich," a balding, middle-aged man says.

"In a minute," Frannie says to the customer. She turns to Grace. "You go to that party and have a nice time. And remember what I told you."

She wags a gloved finger at Grace.

"Be strong," Frannie says as she wraps the sandwich and secures it with tape "Be strong, Grace."

Yes. She has to be strong. But for what? And whom?

Chapter 19
Kitty
3:15 p.m.

People are gathering purses and backpacks, stirring and stretching, impatient to board the flight. Kitty retrieves her boarding pass from her purse and stands up, painfully aware once again of her creaky knees. She walks slowly to the end of the line of passengers waiting to board.

Above the din of the boarding announcement, chattering passengers, and background music, she hears shouts. "Mom!" and "Grandma Kitty!" She turns and sees Claire, Joe, and Skye hurrying toward her. Claire's face is tense with worry, Joe strides behind her with a baffled expression, and Skye trots beside them, waving at her.

Oh, dear. She had wanted to slip quietly away, but, apparently, Claire had found and read her letter, and now there's going to be a tense conversation, tears perhaps, and maybe a plea to keep her from going, which will *not* change her mind.

"Mom, what you are doing?" Claire says, panting, as she reaches Kitty. She hugs her. "I can't believe you were going without saying good-bye!"

"I thought it would be easier this way, dear." Kitty says untangling herself from her daughter's embrace.

"Mom!" Claire looks at Kitty and her eyes fill with tears. "You should have told me. What if something happened to you!"

Kitty sighs. "You're right, Claire. I should have told you. But I thought you'd talk me out of it." She squeezes her daughter's hand. "Now it's done, dear. I've got my ticket, and my plane is boarding. Say good-bye and don't worry."

She is using, she realizes, the same tone of voice she used with Claire when they said goodbye to Mike at the station thirty-four years ago. Kitty had pulled Claire aside and said to her, *Now dry your tears. We don't want Mike's last glimpse of us from the train window to be us crying, do we?*

Joe clears his throat. "We're excited for you, Kitty. We're just concerned."

"I'm fine, truly I am," Kitty says, softening her tone. The boarding announcement crackles over the loudspeaker again. "Agnes and I have it all planned. We have our maps, Agnes has AAA membership, and her son brought the car in for a tune-up last week. We'll be fine."

Claire opens her purse, pulls out a photo, and thrusts it in Kitty' hand. "I grabbed this from the fridge door. Something to remind you of us."

She looks at the photo, taken last Christmas of her with Claire, Joe, and the girls in front of their tree.

"Thank you, Claire," she says, touched by the photo. She tucks it into her purse.

"Grandma, it sounds exciting!" Skye pipes up. She looks at Kitty, her eyes sparkling with excitement. "Send us postcards from every park, okay?"

She hugs her granddaughter. "I will, Skye. I promise."

"And I'll water your flowers," Skye adds. "Every other day like you do."

The ticket agent announces the boarding call again with a tone of firm politeness. Thank goodness. She can finally be on her way. She's glad that her family is seeing her off after all, but it would have been easier if she could have slipped away like she'd planned.

Claire hugs her again. "Mom, have a good trip. Please be careful! Call us—collect—every evening."

"Or every other evening!" Joe adds, looking alarmed, no doubt, at the cost of all those collect calls.

"I'll call every three days, how's that?" she says to Joe. He nods and pats her shoulder.

As the line inches forward, Claire embraces her one more time, and then the three of them step to the side. Kitty feels the tension ease out of her shoulders. That didn't go as badly as she had feared. Claire did not try to persuade her to stay home. Perhaps she should have told Claire and Vivian in advance instead of trying to quietly leave. Maybe Claire had a point: she simply didn't want to be shut out. Kitty resolves that she will send her daughters not only postcards, but letters, too, from every park to make them feel like they are part of her adventure.

She hands her boarding pass to the agent and turns and looks back at Claire, Joe, and Skye one last time. Claire is crying, but she smiles through her tears. Joe wraps his arm around his wife's shoulder, kisses her forehead, and waves.

"Bye, Grandma! Don't forget to write!" Skye calls.

For a moment, Kitty wonders if she's doing the right thing. Claire looks so forlorn. Then she thinks of Mike who is not there to wave goodbye, and who never had the chance to visit a national park, marry, or have children, and of Frederick, who never enjoyed a single day of retirement, and she knows she's doing the right thing.

She can almost hear Mike say, *Have a good trip, Mom. Go on your adventure.* And Frederick saying, *Kitty, let's go!*

She straightens her shoulders and steps onto the plane. Now her adventure begins.

No one is there when Grace gets home from work, which surprises her, because she had figured Mom would be in the kitchen, making appetizers or fruit salad, and Dad would be in the yard, setting out chairs or edging the grass, and Skye would be doing one of her Skye things like scribbling in her diary, or lying on the porch swing with her nose stuck in a book. Dad's VW is gone from the driveway, but she sees her parents' Buick in the garage when she parks her bike.

Yet the house is empty and Honey is prancing by the back door, eager to go outside. The wooden cutting board, covered with bits of cucumber, lies on the counter. She sees a note thumbtacked to the bulletin board by the phone: *Going to airport to see Grandma Kitty, will explain later, love, Mom.*

Grace stared at the note, puzzled. Was Grandma Kitty going someplace? Wouldn't Grandma Kitty have told them? Are they picking someone up at the airport?

If it really was an emergency, she reasons, Mom would have called her at work. If it's not an emergency, then there's no reason to worry about it. Mom will explain when she gets back.

She lets Honey outside and decides to help Mom with the appetizers. She opens the refrigerator door and sees a half-sliced cucumber and a package of cream cheese. A bag of rye bread is on the counter. She'll make the cream cheese and cucumber sandwiches for Mom, and after she's done, maybe she'll go to that open house at the Sullivan estate after all, even though the thought of going by herself isn't appealing, and there's no way Ben can take a break from working at his family's restaurant to go with her, not on a busy holiday weekend.

She's spreading cream cheese on slices of rye bread when Honey barks and dashes to the kitchen door, leaping up and pressing her paws against the screen door. She glances out the window and sees a car pulling in the driveway. It isn't Dad's VW, but a peach-colored Mustang convertible, Aunt Vivian's car. The top is down, and Aunt Vivian is at the wheel. A man is sitting next to her. Interesting. Mom didn't say anything about Aunt Vivian bringing a date. As they get out of the car, the man takes Aunt Vivian's hand to help her, and although Aunt Vivian is not the type of take help from anyone, she smiles at the man, who is tall and handsome in an old-guy way. Grace opens the screen door to let them in.

Aunt Vivian looks stylish, as usual. She was wearing a lime green and white floral print sleeveless shift and has a white cardigan draped over her arm. Her auburn hair is loosely tied back with a bright green and yellow scarf. Grace likes how Aunt Vivian still wears her hair long, instead of clipped in a smooth bob like Mom or sprayed in a helmet hairdo like Grandma Kitty and Grandma Edna.

"Grace, dear, so lovely to see you," Aunt Vivian hugs Grace, and she gets a whiff of her Chanel cologne, which Grace has vowed to buy when she is older and can afford it. It smells so much more sophisticated than Mom's Jean Nate or her own Love's Baby Soft perfume.

"This is Greg, an old friend who's moved back to Wisconsin from California," Aunt Vivian says.

"It's nice to meet you," Grace says and she shakes his hand. His name sounds familiar—didn't Uncle Mike have a friend name Greg? She vaguely remembers Mom mentioning once something about Aunt Vivian breaking his heart.

"Where's your mother, dear?"

Grace shrugs. "Mom left a note saying they were going to get Grandma Kitty at the airport, and she would explain when they got home. I guess Dad and Skye went with her. They're not here, either."

"The airport!" Aunt Vivian says. "What on earth?"

"I don't know, maybe Grandma Kitty is taking a trip. But she never said anything about it."

"Taking a trip. But to where?" Aunt Vivian looks perplexed.

"We can go to the airport and find out what's going on," Greg suggests.

Aunt Vivian considers this, then shakes her head. "No, we may miss them and add to the confusion. The best thing is to wait. Your mom will explain when she gets back," Aunt Vivian adds briskly. "We're here early, so now how can we help?"

A few minutes later, Aunt Vivian is slicing a wedge of cheddar cheese and Grace is placing cheddar squares on crackers, while Greg is busy outside setting up the croquet set.

"Greg seems nice," Grace says.

"Yes, he's very nice."

"How do you know him?" She thinks she knows how, but she doesn't want to say in case she's wrong.

"He's an old friend from high school. He was friends with your Uncle Mike."

"Is he the one who you were engaged to?" Grace blurts out. She can't stand it any longer. She wants to hear the story.

Aunt Vivian turns to her and smiles. "I see your mom has told you about my past romance."

"She mentioned you were engaged to someone once," Grace says. "Greg, right?"

"I think that's enough cheese," Vivian says crisply. She glances over at Grace and arches her eyebrows. "And that's all I'm going to say for now."

"Would you and Greg like to go to an open house with me at the Sullivan Center?" Grace asks to change the subject. Besides, it would be fun to go with Aunt Vivian and Greg. "Heidi gave me tickets. She got them at work, but she can't go, some stupid thing she has to go to with her boyfriend. It's music, I guess, and food. It's only two tickets, but maybe they'll let all three of us in."

"That sounds lovely. I remember going to the—"

The phone rings. Honey barks wildly as she always does when the phone rings, and Grace reaches over the counter to grab the receiver.

"Grace?"

"Hi, Mom. What's going on?"

"We're at the airport. Mitchell, I mean, not O'Hare."

"What's going on?"

"Grandma Kitty decided to fly to Colorado to visit her friend Agnes, but she didn't tell us. Skye stopped at her house this afternoon and found a letter she had left. We barely made it here to say goodbye!"

Mom sounds like she's about to cry.

"They are going to visit the national parks," Mom adds. "She'll be gone for two months."

Grace absorbs this news. She can't picture Grandma Kitty, who she has never seen in anything other than a dress and a string of pearls, hiking through a park.

"Are you okay, Mom? Is Grandma Kitty okay?"

"We'll tell you when we get home, sweetie."

Grace glances over at Aunt Vivian. "Grandma Kitty is flying to Colorado."

Aunt Vivian raises her eyebrows and motions to Grace to hand her the phone.

"Aunt Vivian is here. She wants to talk to you."

"Tell her we'll fill her in when we get home."

"Okay. Uh, Aunt Vivian brought a friend."

"Really? Who?"

"Uh, Greg. Greg . . . uh," Grace glance at her aunt.

"Wright," Aunt Vivian whispers.

"Wright."

"Greg!"

She glanced at Aunt Vivian who smiles and shakes her head and mouths *no*.

"Aunt Vivian says she'll explain," Grace twists the phone cord around her finger. "Listen, we might go to the open house at the Sullivan Center. Heidi gave me tickets."

"Don't stay too long, then. See you later, honey."

Grace hangs up the phone and turns to Aunt Vivian.

"Mom sounded surprised when I mentioned Greg."

Aunt Vivian laughs. "Oh, I'm sure she was."

After they rinse the dishes and put the appetizers in the refrigerator, Grace quickly changes into a buttery yellow sundress, her favorite dress for summer, while Aunt Vivian freshens up in the powder room. Grace runs a comb through her hair and swipes on some pink lip gloss. She studies her reflection. Her nose is shiny and her face is flushed from the heat. Well, so what? She's not going to try to meet someone. Is she? She has a wonderful boyfriend, at least for now, whom she loves. But that doesn't mean she can't look nice at a party. She dabs some powder on her nose to soak up the shine and fluffs her hair.

They take Aunt Vivian's car to the reception. Greg gallantly insists that she sit in front with Vivian, while he wedges himself in the tiny back seat.

Grace feels glamorous in the Mustang convertible. She slips on her sunglasses, and in her sundress and wide straw hat, she feels like she should be in southern California—or southern France, where, she realizes with a start, she will be in eight weeks.

Claire stares at the passing landscape. Outside of Milwaukee, it's all farmland and fields, weathered farmhouses, rows of corn and cabbage.

Her emotions are churning. She's worried about her mother, angry at her for leaving on this adventure. And envious? Is she envious of her mother heading on a two-month jaunt? *Well, yes,* she admits to herself. And hurt, too, that Mom didn't tell her. *I was afraid you would persuade me not to go,* Mom had said. Probably Claire would have tried to talk her out of it. It is a risky venture for two elderly women. But she might have helped her. She could have gone shopping with Mom for clothes—did she bring the right clothes? Did she bring a sun hat? A pair of sturdy hiking shoes? She doesn't know because Mom told her nothing about this trip. The two of them could have looked at maps and hotel brochures together.

The secretive way Mom planned her trip without mentioning a word to her brings back the painful memory of how Mom and Dad shut her out after Mike died. She remembers them whispering in the hallway to friends and stopping abruptly when she appeared, Dad sitting in a study staring at a letter and quickly folding it when she entered the room. They had tried to protect her from grief, and yet all it did was to keep the grief pressed down inside her, and now Mom's adventure was something else withheld from her.

"I wonder why she waited so long," Joe remarks. "She should have done this fifteen years ago."

"I don't know," Claire says. "Maybe she wasn't ready, so soon after Dad died."

Joe shakes his head. "But life's too short to wait." He reaches out and squeezes her hand. "Tell you what, let's go somewhere next summer. You and me and Skye, and Grace if she wants to go, too. Maybe we could go to the Grand Canyon or maybe even Montana. What are we waiting for?"

"I want to go to the Grand Canyon!" Skye chimes in from the back. "Let's go next summer!"

Yes, Claire thinks, life's too short to wait. She thinks about the empty store downtown, the conversation with Gil Romero. Yes, life is too short. What is she waiting for?

The Sullivan estate is a ten-minute drive from the house. Aunt Vivian knows the way by heart, due to going to so many parties and gatherings there as a child and young woman. She drives along the winding road overlooking Lake Michigan, past the lighthouse and around the curve, and turns into the entrance. The name, Sullivan Conference Center, is etched on a bronze sign affixed to one of the stone pillars flanking the entrance. Metal gates with a geometric design open to a long, curving driveway leading to the home, an expansive, T-shaped, prairie style brick ranch home. It's built out of creamy brick with a dark flat roof and floor-to-ceiling windows in the living room.

They park on the vast lawn rapidly filling up with cars. Young men in orange vests are directing people where to park. Aunt Vivian expertly slides in between a tan Cadillac Seville and white Buick LeSabre.

"You haven't lost your touch, Vivian," Greg says as they clamber out of the car. "I remember how well you drove your dad's tank of a Buick."

Aunt Vivian laughs. "He fretted every time I backed it out of the driveway."

Across the lawn, small round white tables and chairs are scattered across the lush lawn, and waiters in black pants and white shirts glide among the clusters of guests with trays of appetizers and drinks.

They stop by a large white tent with a raised wooden floor and peer inside. A long table covered with a red cloth is laden with platters of sandwiches, bowls of salad, plates of fresh fruit, and trays of cookies and brownies. An ice sculpture of the number "200" is melting in the heat.

A plump, petite woman with short brown hair wearing a red satin halter dress sings something smooth and jazzy in front of a trio of a drummer, saxophonist, and a guitar player. Her dark curls bounce around her face as she twirls and sings "Oh-boo-bop." Several couples dance on the polished wood floor in front of the stage, twirling and spinning to the catchy tune.

"This is quite the event," Greg remarks. "I almost expect to see Edmund and Annabelle standing at the door, greeting their guests."

"Their daughter is on the foundation's board, and I'm sure she insisted that the event was up to her parents' standards," Aunt Vivian says.

A young woman balancing a tray of flutes of champagne stops and offers them each a glass.

"I always loved this place," Aunt Vivian says as she takes a flute of champagne and hands one to Grace.

Greg nods. "Me too," he says.

They look at each other and smile, sharing a private memory.

Grace wonders what memory they are silently sharing. Like so much of Aunt Vivian's life, it's a mystery. Her aunt has always been someone who pops in at birthday parties and at Christmas, and when she and Skye were little, sometimes Mom would take them to Aunt Vivian's house for the day, where Aunt Vivian would let them try on her hats and gloves. But she doesn't know her in the same way that she knows Grandma Kitty, or Grandma Edna before she started getting forgetful. Mom told her that Aunt Vivian broke the heart of Uncle Mike's best friend, who apparently is now back in her life, standing next to her, looking not at all brokenhearted. It's confusing, Grace thinks. If she and Ben broke up, she couldn't imagine them ever being friends twenty-five years later. Ever. It would hurt too much.

"Did you come here often?" Grace asks, curious.

"Hmm. A few times a year. For parties."

"What kind of parties? Wild parties?" Grace asks hopefully.

Aunt Vivian laughs "No, not wild, unless you consider a keg of beer and a little canoodling wild.

Alex would invite the entire class every year for an end-of-year school picnic, and his family would host a big party the day after Christmas. The Boxing Day fest they called it."

"Was Alex's family snobbish?"

Aunt Vivian smiled. "Not at all. Alex's father had humble origins. He was a milkman before he started selling powdered milk."

"And maybe other things" Greg adds dryly.

Grace turns to him, puzzled.

Aunt Vivian waves her hand. "Now Greg, I've never believed those bootlegging rumors."

Greg grins. "I'm just saying he made his fortune awfully fast."

"But in any case," Aunt Vivian says, steering the conversation away from bootlegging, "They were a lovely family and their parties were spectacular."

"What were they like?" Grace asks. "Was it like, you know, *The Great Gatsby* with people dancing on tables and drinking until dawn?"

Aunt Vivian laughs. "Oh, no, not like that."

"The house was decked out in evergreen boughs and red velvet bows," Aunt Vivian continues. "We'd spend the afternoon skating on the pond and snowshoeing through the woods, and then everyone would go inside and warm up by the fire and drink hot cocoa. We'd change into our evening clothes, have dinner, and then a band would play and we'd dance for hours."

"Bands would come in from Milwaukee or Chicago," Greg adds. "Mr. Sullivan would hire them for the week, and they'd have parties here every night between Christmas and New Year's."

Grace imagines women in long dresses and men in tuxedos and a band playing the big band music that her parents like to listen to. The parties Aunt Vivian and Greg are describing sound glamorous and so different from what she and Ben and their friends usually do when they have parties, listening to the Eagles or Fleetwood Mac, drinking cans of Old Style or paper cups of Lambrusco wine, and maybe passing around a joint. Even dressing up is different now—when she and Ben went to prom two years ago, he wore a powder-blue tuxedo with a ruffled shirt, and she wore a Gunne Sax calico dress trimmed with velvet and lace. It was pretty, but not at all sexy.

"I think I was born in the wrong era," Grace says.

"Everything was more glamorous back then—the music, the clothes, the movies. I think I like it better now, truthfully," Aunt Vivian says. "Not the dreadful paisley prints or the rock music, of course, but the attitude. Love and peace. Our generation fought in a war; your generation ended one."

"I guess it's hard to see the good in your own time," Grace says. "The seventies. Ugh. I don't think

I'm ever going to look and think this was a great time. Except for being young."

Aunt Vivian and Greg look at each other again and smile.

"Enjoy your youth, Grace," Aunt Vivian says. "Every minute of it."

"I will! *I am*," Grace says. "Well, I'm trying although it's hard sometimes."

"So, why did the family sell the house?" she adds quickly to change the subject. This discussion of enjoying one's youth is getting too serious for her.

"Well," Aunt Vivian frowns. "Alex died in the war. His father could have pulled some strings and got him a position in Washington, but Alex didn't want that. He became a pilot and was shot down over the Pacific."

"It was a big story in the newspaper," Greg says. "*Son of Local Scion Dies as a War Hero*."

"And then they sold the house?"

"His father died a few years after the war—a stroke, I think. I don't think he ever got over Alex's death."

"What about Alex's mother?"

"Annabelle? She lived here for, oh, let's see, I think, twenty years?"

Greg nods. "She died in, what was it, 1962? She left the house and estate to the city to be turned into a conference and event center."

They are quiet for a moment, probably thinking of another private memory.

Greg touches Aunt Vivian's arm. "I see Bob Miller over there. I'll say hello and check out the desserts."

Greg heads toward the tent and waves at a short, balding man in glasses who smiles and claps Greg on the shoulder.

"Greg's nice, Aunt Vivian. I'm glad you connected again," Grace says.

"Yes, I am, too," Aunt Vivian says, blushing. It's cute to see Aunt Vivian blush, Grace thinks.

"Is it weird to be together again?" Grace asks.

Aunt Vivian sips her champagne and nods. "It is, but in a nice way."

Grace looks over at the tent, where an elderly man with thick white hair and a handlebar mustache, dapper in a red and white striped shirt and blue pants, is twirling a slender woman with short, feathered gray hair wearing a long blue and white striped dress and white shoes. He half dips her, pulls her up, and they laugh and hug.

"I'd like that," Grace says, gesturing to the couple. "You know, getting old with someone and dancing together after fifty years."

"They do look sweet," Aunt Vivian says, "but for all you know, they could each be widowed and met each other for the first time today . . . but I know what you mean."

"That young man you would like to grow old with . . . would that be with Ben?' Aunt Vivian adds.

"Well, I . . ." Grace pauses and takes a sip of champagne. "I don't know. I love him, but I'm going to France for a year, and . . ."

"You'd like to be free to fall in love with a handsome young French man, perhaps?" Aunt Vivian asks with a smile, "or perhaps not fall in love with anyone at all?"

"I—I'm not sure. I guess I feel like it's too soon to make that choice," Grace replies. "Ben and I keep arguing about this. He tries to be supportive, and I feel guilty for leaving him, and then I get angry at him, and he gets withdrawn. How do you know you're making the right choice? That you're the right person for them and they are the right person for you?"

"If we could answer that question, there would be no need for novels and poems and songs about love," Aunt Vivian says thoughtfully.

"But what about you? Did you ever regret that you broke up with Greg?" Grace knows that maybe she shouldn't be asking her aunt such a personal question, but the champagne is making her feel daring.

Aunt Vivian looks over at the garden, where a monarch butterfly flutters among the coneflowers and daisies. "It wasn't that I thought I would find anyone better and, frankly, I didn't. I just knew I couldn't be married then."

"Could you have asked Greg to wait for you?"

Aunt Vivian shakes her head. She traces the edge of her champagne glass with her finger before replying.

"I suppose I could have, but I didn't want to keep him in limbo." she says. "After the war, there was a sense of wanting to make up for lost time and get on with things."

"Mom makes it sound like it's tragedy," Grace says. "You know, poor Aunt Vivian, she jilted Greg and never married."

Aunt Vivian laughs. "Oh, no, I'm not a tragic figure. Far from it! I've had a wonderful life so far! If I had truly wanted to marry, I would have. I did have a few chances, you know, no one as sweet as Greg, but I did have my beaus. But I liked my independence more."

"So, you don't want anything to happen with Greg now?" Grace asks. She's confused.

"I'm happy with my life, "Aunt Vivian says. "I have my work, my friends, and two beautiful nieces, one of with whom I'm enjoying this lovely afternoon, dear. And if Greg and I continue to enjoy each other's company—in our own way—well, that would be a delightful surprise, like getting a birthday gift you didn't expect."

"I don't want to choose," Grace cries. "I want it all!" She's feeling a little dizzy from the champagne and the sun and the exhaustion from staying up all night on the beach. She drains her champagne glass and sets it down on a table. She spreads her arms and spins around. "I want it all!"

"Why not? That's what the women's movement is fighting for."

"Then why can't I go to Provence and still have Ben?" Grace says, smoothing the front of her sundress. "Why do I have to choose?"

"What are you afraid will happen if you're apart for a year?"

"Well, you know. We won't see each other for so long, we'll both change, and maybe I'll meet someone."

"And if you do?"

"That's my dilemma!" Grace cries. "What if I don't go to France, and I always regret it, but what if I do go and I regret leaving Ben?"

"Well, there's no easy answer is there?" Vivian arches her eyebrows and looks straight at Grace. "Life is complicated, my dear."'

"I'm beginning to notice," Grace says wistfully.

Behind them, the band switches to a disco song. Couples break apart, and the elderly couple laughs. The man kisses the woman's hand, and they walk hand in hand to the edge of the dance floor and sit down next to each other on two folding chairs.

Greg weaves his way through the crowd, holding a plate heaped with cookies and brownies.

He holds out the plate. "Ladies, take your pick."

Skye runs a comb through her thick, coarse hair. She wishes she had straight, silky hair like Grace and Mom, not unruly wavy hair like Dad. On hot days like today, Mom and Grace twist their hair up in dos they fasten with clips and bobby pins. They look cool and chic. She has tried so many times to fix her hair in the same way, but whenever she tries to twist her hair in a bun or a braid, bits of her hair poke out. She looks ridiculous.

She decides to wear her hair pulled back, so it doesn't fall in her face. Mom says she should wear her hair away from her face to show off her pretty blue eyes, and maybe if she does, Zack will notice her eyes—and her. She thinks about Zack and Jenny laughing together this morning, and she pushes the thought away and instead thinks of Zack winking at her. She'll wear her blue shirt that matches her eyes and maybe Zack will see her, really see her, and not pay any attention to Jenny. Maybe.

As they drive back to the house. Vivian is lost in thought. Grace is leaning back in the seat beside her, eyes closed, and Greg is squeezed in the Mustang's snug back seat. With the wind, it's too hard to talk.

Spending time at the Sullivan estate has brought back memories. She thinks of Greg and Mike's high school graduation party there, Middleport High School Class of 1942. Already so many young men had gone away, so many had been lost. She was a year behind Greg and Mike, only a junior, but she was there as Greg's date. She and Greg had walked around the grounds in the moonlight, holding hands. He told her that he and Mike had decided that they were going to enlist later that week and not wait to be drafted. Mike was joining the Army, and Greg was enlisting in the Navy. She tried to talk Greg out of the decision. *Wait,* she had said. *Please. Maybe the war will be over by the time your number comes up.* But Greg had shook his head and said, *No, they were going. It was better to enlist and choose than to wait to be drafted.*

Greg had dropped her off in the early morning hours. Mike and Maggie, who had left the party before they did, were sitting on the front porch swing. Maggie was crying. The four of them had sat quietly on the porch as the night faded to dawn, and then they had walked to the Caboose Diner and ate waffles and coffee and tried to act like they hadn't a care in the world and were simply four teenagers enjoying breakfast after their graduation party. The next week, Mike and Greg had walked to the enlistment office.

She and Maggie talked about joining the WACs or WAVES, but Maggie had decided that her place was at home, volunteering with the Red Cross and waiting for Mike to return. She didn't want to be stationed in another city, or, worse, somewhere overseas, if Mike came home for leave. What kept Vivian from joining one of the women's auxiliary military services was the haunted look in her mother's eyes. Most likely she would have ended up typing and filing at a base somewhere, but what if she were sent overseas, somewhere where there was fighting and bombing? She couldn't worry her mother like that, so she had worked part-time at Zimmer's department store and taken the train to Milwaukee twice a week to take classes toward her English degree, but after Mike was killed, she headed to Chicago, was hired as a receptionist at an advertising agency, launched her career as a copywriter, and never looked back. She returned to Milwaukee after Dad died and began a freelance career as a copywriter, but when she returned, she was an independent middle-aged career woman, not the wide-eyed girl she had been.

She should have waited until Greg came home or talked to him before leaving. But she hadn't. She had taken the coward's way out by dropping that awful letter into the mailbox, thinking, *That's that, no going back*. She shudders now at her youthful callousness and her heart aches to think of Greg opening the envelope, tired and dirty after hours of caring for wounded men and reading that horrible letter. *I think we should break our relationship off, my darling. The world is uncertain and we don't know how long this will last.*

He deserves better than her. He deserves a sweet widow or divorcee, perhaps, a woman who knows how to cook and keep house and wants nothing more in life other than to be a wife. He deserves better than a spinster who is set in her ways and can barely boil an egg.

She knows herself, knows how much she loves her independence, as well as her tendency to become impatient with the compromises required in a relationship. Was the possibility of a lasting romantic love worth the risk of hurting Greg again? He is a handsome, kind widower, and surely he will find another woman to love, someone who can be a true helpmate to him, someone who never broke his heart.

Maybe the best thing to do is to let him go before she hurts him again.

She sees Joe's VW in the driveway, so she parks on the street. Grace hops out.

"Mom and Dad are back. I'll tell them we're home." She hurries up the driveway.

Greg climbs awkwardly out of the back seat and walks around to the driver's side to open the door for Vivian, but she's staring straight ahead and doesn't notice him. His smile fades.

"Is everything okay? You seem lost in thought."

Vivian turns and looks at him. "Yes. Well, no." She bites her lip.

He exhales. "You're thinking I shouldn't have come."

"No! No, I'm glad you're here." She takes his hand. "Really, I am. It's just that—"

"What?"

"I—oh, never mind."

"Vivian, be straight with me." He looks at her questioningly.

Vivian sighs. "Greg, perhaps—it's best if the past stays in the past." Greg starts to say something, but Vivian hears her name called and turns to see Claire waving from the door. She lets go of his hand, opens the car door, steps out, and kisses Greg on the cheek. "I'm sorry I brought this up. We'll talk about this later. Really."

He nods, but Vivian can see the hurt in his eyes and fears that, once again, she has spoiled it all.

Chapter 25
Kitty
6 p.m.

The pilot announces they are beginning the descent into Denver.

It was a smooth flight. Kitty dozed most of the way. She is in a window seat with the seat next to her free. Across the aisle from her is the rumpled young couple she had seen in the airport. They are both asleep. The girl is curled up in her seat like a kitten, smiling like she's having a lovely dream. The young man slouches in his seat, snoring softly. He reminds her of Mike at that age with his long legs and deep, peaceful sleep.

She peers out the window. The land below is brown and rocky, so different from the gentle green of Wisconsin. Far below, she sees miniature houses and tiny cars on straight highways etched through a dusty landscape.

The plane bumps as it begins to descend, and she grips the armrest. The young man across from her stirs, sits up, runs his hand through his hair. He stretches and looks over at her. He smiles. "It will be okay, ma'am. It's only turbulence."

"Thank you. I know. I haven't flown for many years, that's all."

"Visiting family?"

"An old friend I haven't seen for a long time."

"My girlfriend and I are visiting her parents in Denver."

"How nice," Kitty says. "Have a good holiday."

She smiles at him politely to end the conversation and turns back to the view out the window. He really is a pleasant young man, despite his scruffiness, but she doesn't want to chat right now. She's too excited to make small talk. She can't believe she is almost there. Agnes and Scott are meeting her at the airport. After a few days of rest with Scott's family, she and Agnes will climb in her station wagon and set out together for Zion, Bryce, and the Grand Canyon, then up to Yellowstone and Glacier, and back to Denver. They will be two old ladies—two old friends—on perhaps their last adventure together.

She can't wait.

It was a surprise when Vivian showed up with Greg. As Claire sets plates and silverware rolled into red, white, and blue napkins on the table for a buffet supper, she finds herself feeling irritated at her sister. Vivian had mentioned casually a few weeks ago that Greg had moved back to Wisconsin, called her, and they had met for lunch.

"How did it go? She had asked her sister, worried that this meeting might have stirred up painful memories for Vivian.

"It went fine," Vivian had said, and then filled her in on the death of Greg's wife, poor Maggie. Claire had always liked her, a quiet girl who had complemented Mike's gregariousness. It had been a surprise—or perhaps not—when Maggie quickly married Greg. Claire had felt resentful at first that Maggie had forgotten her brother so soon, but when she herself grew up and married Joe her feelings had mellowed, and she understood that Maggie grieving for Mike for years as a lonely spinster would have accomplished absolutely nothing.

After that conversation, Claire had talked to Vivian briefly a few times in the next couple of weeks. Vivian had sounded distracted, which she had attributed to a backlog of copywriting assignments, and Claire had refrained from asking any more about Greg. And now—surprise!—they were an item and had apparently worked through the awkwardness of their broken engagement.

She stirs the fruit salad vigorously. A cherry spills out of the bowl and she sweeps it into the sink.

It's not that she isn't happy for Vivian—and Greg—she is, although she wonders how long this might last. Rather, it is that, once again, Vivian is breezing into her life without considering how Claire might feel about things.

She pushes aside the jealously she sometimes feels toward her sister and turns her thoughts to the old appliance resale shop downtown, the televisions jammed precariously on top of one another, the business card tucked in her purse, the name that had popped into her head: HerArt, a Creative Coffee Shop. She sees it so clearly in her mind. She sees the walls painted creamy white again, like when it was Svenson's Home Goods. She sees the sunlight pouring through the windows, the hardwood floor cleaned and polished, the wooden chairs and tables painted blue and red and yellow, the laughter and hum of conversation as women sip coffee together, the colorful artwork and photographs covering the walls.

"Honey, where's the cribbage board?" Joe says, walking into the kitchen. "I thought Greg and I could play a game."

"It's in the hall closet," Claire says absently.

He rummages in the closet and returns to the kitchen holding a board and cards.

"Thinking about your mom?"

"Yes, no, well, yes,"

"She'll be fine."

"I hope so. I feel a little better after talking with Agnes's son."

"And?" Joe tilts his head and smiles at her. "Anything else on your mind?"

"Well," Claire takes a deep breath. "I was thinking that Middleport needs an art gallery. Downtown."

"Oh." Joe looks at her quizzically. "An art gallery?"

Claire plunges ahead. "The old junk shop that used to be Svenson's. I ran into the owner's son. His dad has retired and he's looking for a new tenant for the space."

"And?"

Claire pauses and then says, "I was thinking of . . . renting it. With some of the money I've saved, and the nest egg from Dad's life insurance—I know that's our emergency fund, but the rent would be next to nothing. Gil Romero said he simply wants someone to take over the space so it's not sitting empty. I was thinking of maybe turning it into—I'm not sure exactly what. A coffee shop and an art gallery. Both. A place for women to meet and drink coffee and display their paintings and photographs."

Joe is quiet for a moment. "Like your ladies book club, but official," he says.

"Well, yes, sort of."

"But sweetie, who goes downtown anymore?" he says doubtfully. "Wouldn't the mall be a better place for something like that? And you said you wanted to get an air conditioner next year and—"

"You're right," she says quickly. "It's a silly idea. Never mind."

Joe sighs. "Claire, don't shut me out. Look, let's talk about it after the weekend. Maybe we should wait until things are more settled. I might be changing jobs, we were thinking of visiting Grace next spring, Skye will be starting college in five years . . ."

"Fine. Forget I said anything," Claire snaps. "I get it, there are more important things to spend money on right now."

"It's your money. Do what you want. But it's downtown!" Joe adds. "Who wants to be downtown? It's dying, Claire. It's not a practical place to start a business."

"I want to be downtown! And you're not being supportive!" She feels her cheeks flush. They are getting into an argument at the worst possible time. She lowers her voice. Greg is on the porch and Vivian is in the powder room, and she doesn't want them to overhear their argument. She knows he has a point. This is not the time to even think about doing something as risky as opening a new business, and what does she know about running a coffee shop? Absolutely nothing. The nest egg should be used for something more important than an idea in her head. And yet, she can't let go of it: A place for women to gather, away from their families and obligations, a place of their own.

Joe studies her face for a moment. Then he nods and says, "Let's talk about it tomorrow morning, okay?"

She nods and turns back to her work. A conversation tomorrow. It's a start.

Grace spreads cold cream on her face, grabs a tissue, and wipes it off. She's flushed and sweaty from being in the sun at the open house at the Sullivan estate, so she's going to redo her makeup—not much, only a little mascara, powder, and lip gloss.

There's a knock on the door. "Grace? Are you almost done?"

Grace rolls her eyes at the sound of her little sister's voice and yanks open the door.

"What!" She doesn't mean to snap, but Skye bothers her at the most inconvenient times.

"Um, does this look okay?" She looks at Grace anxiously. Skye is wearing jean shorts and a red tank top beneath a blue linen blouse buttoned almost to her chin. Her hair is tightly pulled back with bobby pins that make her look like she's five years old and off to kindergarten.

Grace feels her mood soften. Her brainy sister doesn't often ask her advice on anything. She studies Skye thoughtfully.

"Unbutton your shirt a couple of buttons, so it's open over your tank, not buttoned up like you're at church," she tells Skye. "And try this with your hair." She takes out the bobby pins, expertly twists back a strand of Skye's hair on each side of her face, and loosely fastens each strand with the bobby pins. "There, see? Your hair is off your face, but softer, more sophisticated. Not like a schoolteacher."

Skye touches her hair and peers around Grace's shoulder to look in the mirror.

"That does look better! Thanks, Grace."

Grace resists the urge to ruffle her sister's hair, like she did when Skye was six years old. She's not six anymore, and she kind of feels sorry for her sister because she thinks high school is going to be hard for her. Not the books, but everything else.

"Happy to help." She gently nudges Skye out the door. "Now if you don't mind, I was in the middle of washing my face."

Vivian has retreated to the powder room to freshen up. She brushes her hair and pulls out a strand of gray—she's not yet coloring her hair, but she's considering it. While men look handsome with gray hair—Greg, for instance—she fears gray locks will push her into the category of grandmotherly, which she is not yet ready to move into, thank you very much.

She applies fresh lipstick and pats powder on her nose. She's glad for this moment of quiet. Joe and Greg are playing a game of cribbage, and Claire is busy in the kitchen and, of course, refusing any help. Her emotions are churning. She knows Claire is—well, not disapproving, exactly, but not entirely pleased that she's reconnected with Greg. It's almost as if—she thinks as she tucks her lipstick back into her makeup bag—she's not supposed to have both a career and a beau. It's like she has to choose.

It's funny, she thinks, how each of them presumes the other has had it better. Claire thinks Vivian has it easy because she doesn't have any children, while she envies the cocoon of support and love that comes with a spouse and children. She has to do a delicate dance. She has to be the doting aunt, which is easy because she adores her nieces, yet not upstage Claire in any way. "You get all the fun, I get all the work," Claire had said snappishly after a few gin and tonics when they'd gotten together on Memorial Day.

She opens the door and bumps into Skye. Her hair is pulled back off her face, and Vivian catches a whiff of Jean Nate.

"Grace is in the other bathroom," Skye says as way of explanation.

"Oh, I'm done," She smiles at her niece. "That was quite an adventure this afternoon."

Skye nods. "Yeah, it sounds fun for Grandma Kitty! Mom is worried, but I think it's cool they're going on an adventure."

She looks at her niece. "You look lovely," she ventures cautiously.

Skye is thirteen now, and in the past year her niece has blossomed from a gawky girl to a teenager. She both pities and envies Skye. She fears that adolescence will be hard for Skye, who is smart and curious, but socially awkward, unlike Grace who sailed unperturbed through high school, or at least unperturbed on the surface. Their conversation this afternoon convinced her that Grace is like a swan, serenely gliding above the water but paddling furiously below.

"Jenny and I are going to see the Middleport Junior High Jazz Band at the park," Skye says. "No big deal."

"Do you have any friends in the band?" Vivian asks.

Skye blushes. "Just a guy in my history class this summer."

"Oh, the Bicentennial movie?" Vivian recalls Claire telling her on the phone about Skye's summer school project and *a pint-sized Francis Ford Coppola.* Much drama, she recalls, and a boy named Jack? No, Zack, and Claire suspects Skye likes him.

"Do I look okay?" Skye asks anxiously.

Of course she does. She's beautiful because she's young and all young people are beautiful, but they are too self-conscious and self-absorbed to realize it. Youth is truly wasted on the young, Vivian thinks.

"I asked Grace and she said I looked okay," Skye says. "She always looks nice," Skye adds. "Her hair never gets frizzy, and she and Mom know how to do their hair and stuff. Grace always looks perfect. I will never be like that."

Vivian bites her lip to keep from laughing. An hour ago at the open house, Grace was confiding to her that "Skye can be as weird as she wants, and I have to be Miss Perfect," and now Skye is telling her that, "Grace is always perfect." How did Claire do it—two girls! How did her own mother do it?

"Well," she says. "Just be yourself, find your own style."

"But I don't know who I am!" Skye says. "Like what's my style? Jenny said I have to find my style, but I don't even know what it is. I like blue, and I don't like ruffly clothes, but I don't know what clothes to wear or stuff like that."

Vivian brushes a stand of hair out of Skye's eyes. "You will. I could take you shopping, maybe in Chicago if you'd like. We could take the train and go to that new Water Tower Place mall and shop at Marshall Fields. Now, shall we see if your mom needs any help?"

"You okay, Mom?" Skye asks.

Claire has been lost in thought, gazing out the window at the sparrows fluttering around the birdfeeder, thinking of her mother, up in the air somewhere over the plains. She turns to her daughter, who has followed Vivian into the kitchen.

"I'm fine, sweetheart. It was just a shock to find out that Grandma was flying to Colorado."

Skye shrugs. "I guess she wanted an adventure."

"If she had told us, we could have helped her plan it."

"Yes, that would have been helpful," Vivian adds tartly. She looks at Claire and nods. At least for this, Claire thinks, they are in agreement.

Claire scoops some turkey, cheese, and fruit salad on a plate. She hands it to Skye, who rolls her eyes. "Mom, I'm not hungry."

"Eat something!" Claire and Vivian say in unison.

Claire looks at her sister, who smiles at her. Usually, Claire would be annoyed with Vivian butting in, but at this moment she's glad to have the reinforcement.

Skye eats a few bits of cheese and sets down the plate. "Okay. I ate." She heads toward the door. "Bye!"

"Was I like that as a teenager?" Claire remarks to Vivian, as the screen door slams shut.

"I don't know, actually." Vivian says. "I wasn't there."

A memory flashes into Claire's mind of sitting on the edge of Vivian's bed watching her pack a suitcase. She pushes aside the thought.

"Well, you're here now," she says briskly.

Vivian nods, and Claire sees something like gratitude in her eyes.

"What can I do to help?" Vivian asks.

The concert is starting in five minutes. First the Middleport Junior High Jazz Band will play, then the Middleport High School Jazz Band, and then, at the end, the Middleport Municipal Band.

Skye and Jenny are walking across the dusty grass to the green and white gazebo in the middle of Lakeview Park. Skye has applied Bonne Bell lip gloss and dabbed some of Mom's Coty face powder on her nose to cover the shine. She's glad Grace told her to wear her shirt loose because she probably would have looked dorky with it buttoned up. Jenny is wearing blue jean shorts that barely cover her butt, a red tube top, and big hoop earrings. Skye thinks it's too much, like she's trying to look like she's eighteen, but maybe that's what boys like? She'll ask Grace, she decides, who always looks like she stepped out of the pages of *Seventeen* magazine. Usually, Grace treats her like she's just her annoying little sister, but she was nice to her today with the advice about her hair and top, and maybe if she asks Grace for help with her clothes, she will give her some more suggestions before she leaves for France, and she can write them in her journal so she remembers. She could ask Mom, too, but Mom's idea of what looks nice is old-fashioned, from the 1950s, and besides, Mom would tell her she's too young to think about boys.

"Billy was a dweeb about the beer," Jenny says. "It was a joke."

"He could have gotten in trouble," Skye says. She feels like she has to stick up for Billy. "And we could have, too."

Jenny shrugs. "Billy is a goody two-shoes. Zack thought it was funny."

"But what if Billy's parents find out?"

"What if they don't?" Jenny retorts. "God, you're such a worry wart, Skye!"

Skye doesn't reply. She doesn't want to fight with Jenny and maybe she's right. Maybe she is too uptight. It was funny to see Billy spit out the beer like that. She glances at Jenny. Some older boys walking by do a doubletake at Jenny and whistle. "Hey, cutie!" Jenny smiles and tosses her hair. Skye notices that the guys didn't even glance at her.

Sometimes she doesn't even like Jenny that much, Skye realizes with a start, even though she's been her best friend since third grade. They used to play with their Barbies and lie on the floor watching *Electric Company* and *Zoom*. Jenny always wanted to hang around with her then, dropping hints to stay for supper. Mom didn't mind and would give Jenny a bag of cookies to take home. Sometimes Jenny would invite her to her house, but she never liked going there. Her dad was always sleeping because he worked third shift at a factory, and her mom would sit in the living room, smoking cigarettes, drinking beer, and watching game shows while she and Jenny ate TV dinners in the kitchen. She used to feel kind of sorry for Jenny, but Jenny's changed a lot and is sometimes mean to her, so she doesn't feel sorry for her anymore.

"Skye, come on, pokey!"

The gazebo is decorated with red, white, and blue crepe paper taped to the railings. A big sign hanging from the roof says, "Middleport Junior High and High School Bicentennial Eve Jazz Concert." All around the gazebo, people are sitting on striped lawn chairs and sprawled out on plaid blankets. Behind the gazebo, a white canopy tent is set up where band members are gathering before they perform.

"C'mon let's sit up front where Zack can see us." Jenny elbows her way through the crowd and finds a spot between a couple lying on a blanket and an old lady in a lawn chair. Jenny flops down on the grass. Skye sits gingerly beside her. She should have brought a blanket. She'll have dirt on the bottom of her shorts when she stands up.

Jenny turns to her. "You know," she says. "You and Billy are cute together. You're so much alike. "

Skye feels her cheeks get hot. "No, we're not."

"Yeah, you are." Jenny nudges her. "You're both really smart and goody-two-shoes about stuff, you're *perfect* together."

"No, we're not!" Skye says. "We're not." She doesn't want to be paired up with Billy.

Jenny shrugs. "You sure were upset today about the beer. I thought it was hilarious! Zack did, too."

Skye opens her month to say something, although she's not sure what, so she shrugs and says, "Whatever."

The Middleport Junior High Jazz Band walks on the stage and the kids sit down on the metal folding chairs. Zack is sitting two rows back. He looks over at them. Jenny shouts "Hey, Zack!" and Skye waves. He looks at them and grins and holds up his saxophone.

The band launches into a jazzy rendition of *Stars and Stripes.* The crowd claps and a couple of little kids in the first row stand up and dance, waving tiny American flags.

The song sounds like the *Stars and Stripes* Skye has heard before, but different, too. Maybe love is like that, Skye thinks. It's the stuff you know, like going to the movies or hanging out with friends, but it's got a different rhythm to it. The same, but not the same.

The band ends with *Yankee Doodle Dandy*. The crowd applauds, and Skye glances over and sees Zack's mom and grandparents clapping and smiling proudly. She looks back at the stage. Zack sees her, smiles, and gives her a thumbs up, and she feels her cheeks get warm. She hates that she blushes so easily.

Jenny taps her on the shoulder. "I have to use the bathroom. Be right back."

The Middleport Junior High Jazz Band heads offstage. Skye waits for Jenny, but she doesn't come back. When the Middleport High School Jazz Band files on stage she decides to see if Jenny is stuck waiting in line. She crosses the park to the bathroom and sees a line of women and girls waiting to use the restroom, but she doesn't spot Jenny. She squeezes past the women in line, apologizing, saying, "I'm just looking for my friend." She pokes her head in the doorway.

"Jenny?" she calls.

"Not me!" someone cries out.

Maybe she missed her while walking over. Skye walks back to the gazebo, where the next band is now performing something that she remembers from music class might be Aaron Copeland. She doesn't see Jenny there, either. She walks over to the tent where the bands gather before and after playing. Maybe she can say hi to Zack. She spots him near the tent and stops. He's standing next to Jenny, who is giggling. She tosses her hair and Zack leans over, brushes her hair away from her face, and whispers something in her ear.

Skye turns around and walks quickly away. Tears burn her eyes. She feels like an idiot. Zack doesn't like her and he will never like a girl like her.

"Skye, wait up!"

Skye turns and sees Zack jogging toward her awkwardly holding his saxophone in one hand.

"Why are you leaving?" He looks hurt.

"Um, I have to get back."

"Hey, thanks for coming."

"Sure." She looks down so Zack won't see the tears in her eyes, and she scuffs the toe of her sneaker in the grass.

"Skye," Zack touches her shoulder and she looks up at him. He glances back at Jenny, who is still standing by the tent, hands on her hips, and then he turns back to her.

"Look, I like Jenny. She's cool and a lot of fun." He pauses. "And I like you, too. Can't we all be friends? Geez, why does everything have to get weird and so complicated?"

"Nothing's complicated," Skye says. Now she feels like a dork for being upset. "I don't feel complicated about anything."

"Friends?" Zack holds out his hand. Skye hesitates and takes it. His palm is dry and warm. She likes how his hand feels wrapped around hers.

She nods. "Friends."

He smiles a smile that lights up his whole face.

"Cool." And then he leans close. Startled, she turns her face away, and his lips brush her cheek.

He steps back and looks at her. "Sorry. I thought you wanted me to do that."

Now Skye's really confused. He sort of kissed her, but he didn't. He likes Jenny, but he likes her, too. He wanted to be friends, but he tried to kiss her. She steps back.

"Look, I've got to go. Tell Jenny I couldn't stay." She hurries away. She wants to look back, but she doesn't. Right now, she hates Jenny for being what guys want, she hates Zack for acting like a jerk, and she hates being thirteen.

Chapter 31
Claire
7:30 p.m.

All the preparations are done. Claire is taking this moment to sit inside the screened-in porch and enjoy a glass of lemonade. Honey dozes by her feet. It's quiet in the house. Vivian and Greg are taking a walk, Grace is in her room, Skye is at the concert, and Joe is in the backyard turning off the sprinkler and winding the hose.

Grace came back from the open house at the Sullivan Center smiling and glowing. Claire hates to admit it to herself, but she's jealous of Vivian and her effect on her girls. Vivian sails in every few months, and the girls think she's wonderful, but Vivian isn't the one who helped them with their homework, made their lunches, and took care of them when they were sick. She wouldn't trade her life and her family for anything, of course, and she's glad that they feel close to their aunt. But still. Did Vivian always have to act so glamorous? And she's miffed at Vivian for keeping her romance with Greg a secret. Why does her sister shut her out like that?

She takes another sip of lemonade and closes her eyes. She thinks back to her conversation earlier in the day with Gil Romero, the dusty junk shop that once had been Svenson's and might be . . . She opens her eyes and shakes her head. *No.* Absolutely not.

Chapter 32
Rob
7:35 p.m.

Rob is dozing on the couch and dreaming that he and his brother Joe are flying in a wooden airplane together. They are boys again, maybe eight and ten, gliding on a current of air as if by magic. His mother is below, hanging out laundry, and pays them no attention. His father sits in a green and white striped lawn chair, drinking a Schlitz. He looks up and waves at them as they soar above him doing a figure eight.

"Have fun, boys!" his father calls up to them.

The sounds of a click and the front door squeaking as it is pushed open jolts him awake. He sits up and rubs his eyes. Amy? A burglar?

"Dad?" He hears his son's voice. "Anyone home?"

He leaps up from the couch and hurries to the front door.

And there is Sam, standing in the foyer, rumpled and sweaty with his canvas backpack on the floor next to him. He needs a haircut, his chin is covered with fine brown stubble, and he's wearing mud-splatted jean cutoffs and a faded, wrinkled T-shirt, the one Amy bought him at the State Fair a few years ago that says "Days of Swine and Roses" with a picture of a pig holding a rose its mouth.

"Sam!" Rob hugs his son. He smells like sweat and dirt and grass.

"We decided to come back a day early. We hitched a ride in the back of a truck for a couple of hours and then biked the last thirty miles."

"Glad you are home, son." Rob says. Although he's alarmed that Sam hitchhiked home, he's not going to mention it now. That's a talk for another time. He's just happy that Sam is back.

"Is Mom home?" Sam asks, looking past his shoulder toward the kitchen.

"Not yet," Rob says. "She's still with Grandpa. He's okay, but he needs some help for a while."

Sam looks crestfallen.

"So how was the trip?" Rob says to move past the subject of Amy's absence.

"It was cool. We saw a lot," Sam says. "We met a couple of girls biking, and we rode with them for a couple of days, too."

There's an awkward silence, and Rob realizes that he's not quite sure how to approach his son now. He left a teenager and came back a young man. It's a cliché, the son growing up suddenly, but Rob understands at this moment that it's a true one.

"Are you hungry?" Rob asks. "There's a frozen pizza in the fridge, or I could grill a couple of burgers.

Then we can go to Aunt Claire and Uncle Joe's if you want to watch the fireworks."

"Burgers would be good," Sam says. "I'm going to take a shower first. I stink."

Rob hugs his son again, watches him head down the hall, toss his backpack in the bedroom. Sam stops and turns back to Rob.

"Dad?" He looks anxiously at Rob. "Mom—she's not coming back, is she?"

Rob hesitates.

"I don't know, Sam," he says after a moment. "I don't know."

"We can talk about it tomorrow," Rob adds quietly. "After you've gotten a good night's sleep."

Sam considers this and nods. "Okay."

Sam pulls off his grimy T-shirt and tosses it in the laundry chute. He slams the chute door shut and Rob resists the urge to say, as he has a hundred times, "Don't shut it so hard."

Sam turns to Rob. "It's good to be home, Dad."

He smiles at his son. "Good to have you home, Sam."

His son is home and for now that is enough.

Chapter 33
Joe
8 p.m.

When Joe was a child, his mother was full of energy, quick to anger, impatient with his father. As difficult as his mother could be, he feels sad as he watches her ease out of Chester's Lincoln Continental, clutching Chester's arm and taking halting steps toward the house. They are an hour late. Chester is always punctual, but he must have struggled to get Mom ready and out the door this evening.

He is struck by how much his mother has withered. Her once-curvaceous figure is spindly, her arms like toothpicks, and her once-lustrous chestnut brown hair, which both he and Rob inherited, is now white and wispy. She reminds Joe of a dandelion that would blow away in a puff of wind.

Mom looks at him blankly and nods, "Hello . . . Joe? Have I been to your house before?"

"Yes, Mom," he says. "You've been to our house many, many times"

The anger he felt toward his mother years ago has faded; now what he feels is sorrow at her decline.

Chester shakes his head. "She's getting worse, but she still has her good days," he whispers to Joe.

It was a surprise twenty years ago when his mother married Claire's Uncle Chester—Kitty's shy younger brother. At first there was awkwardness—Kitty wasn't pleased that her sweet brother was going out with Joe's mother; Claire told him that her mother could not forgive Edna for neglecting her sons. But his mother had brought some sparkle into Chester's life—his mother was nothing if not fun—and Chester and Edna had a good fifteen years together before his mother began to fade.

Chester settles her in a chair on the porch and Grace brings her grandmother a glass of iced tea. In earlier years, Edna would have asked for a martini, but she can't drink now because of her medications and, besides, Joe assumes she doesn't care anymore what she's drinking. Edna smiles vacantly at Claire and drinks her tea, holding the glass carefully in shaking hands. Chester leans over and tenderly wipes her mouth.

Skye comes outside and wanders to the end of the driveway. She had returned from the concert a few minutes ago and went straight to her room. Claire glances at Skye with a worried look and then looks at Joe. "Talk to Skye," she mouths.

He nods, picks up the silver ice bucket on the table and walks to his daughter. "Skye, want to come in the kitchen to help me refill the ice bucket?"

She turns to look at her father and shrugs. "Sure. I guess."

Skye follows her father into the kitchen. Joe opens the freezer and pulls out three metal ice trays. He pushes the lever to release the ice, and the cubes clatter into the bucket. He hands the empty ice tray to Skye. She turns on the faucet and carefully fills the trays with water.

"How was the concert?" he asks.

Skye shrugs. "It was okay, I guess. The band was good."

"Your friend from school—Zachary—is in the band?" He feels like he is thrashing about for a way to talk to her. This is Claire's department, not his, damn it, but she's got her hands full now attending to their guests.

Skye pushes her hair out of her eyes. She looks down at the counter.

"Zack's in the band. But he's not my friend, not really. He's just a guy in my history class. I think he's Jenny's friend, actually," Skye adds. She opens the freezer door and slides in the trays.

"Why do you think he's friends with Jenny and not you?" Joe asks.

Sky shuts the freezer door and turns back to him.

"Well, I know she likes him and I think he likes her, too." She shrugs like she doesn't care, but her face reddens and she bites her lip.

He awkwardly pats her shoulder. He has no idea what to say, but he'll try.

He clears his throat. "You know, when I was in junior high, I had a crush on a girl named Mildred—Millie. She was cute and a cheerleader, and all the boys liked her. If I could get her to look at me and smile, I felt—" he motions like he's throwing a basketball into a hoop "—like I had made the winning score in basketball. And if she didn't—well, I'd mope about all day."

Skye frowns. "How could she not like you, Dad?"

"Every boy was interested in her, and I never quite knew where I stood with her. Sometimes she'd let me hold her books as we walked down the hallway, and other days she'd pretend she didn't know me. I'd be up and down. One day I was in the clouds, the next down in the dumps."

"So what happened?" Skye says.

"I asked her to the spring dance in ninth grade, and she said yes. But the night before the dance she called me and said that she had forgotten that she had said yes to someone else, who turned out to be the ninth-grade class president and star of the basketball team. I don't think she really forgot. I think he asked her after I did and she decided to take a better offer. I was crushed, and avoided her for a week, taking the long way to classes so I wouldn't run into her."

Skye frowns. "She didn't deserve you, Dad. You were better off without her."

"I eventually figured that out. Then I got to know your mom when I started making deliveries for the drugstore. She was always nice to me. When I was home for the summer after my freshman year of college, I was working on the city road crew, and one day I stopped into the drugstore for lunch and there was your mom, helping out at the lunch counter. I remember she was wearing a blue and white checked dress like Dorothy from *The Wizard of Oz*. I fell in love right then and there. We started dating and that was it."

"Did she say yes right away when you asked her out?"

"She did."

"But I thought girls are supposed to play hard to get," Skye says.

"After your Uncle Mike died in the war, I think your mom realized she didn't want to waste her time with silly games. She liked me, I liked her, and neither of us was interested in pretending."

"But how do you know if someone is right for you?"

"Just be your own sweet self and you'll know," Joe tells his daughter. He wishes he had more words or wisdom to offer her for the stormy years ahead, but that's the best advice he can think of now. He kisses his daughter's forehead.

"Just be yourself and don't let anyone make you feel like you're not enough. You are, kiddo, you are."

Greg and Vivian are walking Honey along the bluff overlooking Lake Michigan. The little poodle sniffs the grass, paws at it, then squats and pees.

"Good girl," Greg says.

"I'm surprised you don't have a dog," Vivian says. "You loved our dog. Remember Poppy?"

"That bulldog! She was a sweetheart," Greg says. "I'd feed her scraps under the table when I came over for Sunday dinner."

"Alison begged for a dog," Greg continues, "but Maggie thought she'd end up doing all the work, so she said no. She and David have a cocker spaniel now, Coco."

"And you're a doting grandfather to your granddog, I imagine."

He shakes his head and smiles ruefully. "Yes, I admit to spoiling her. I spent a half hour in the pet store last week looking at chew toys and treats."

Vivian looks out at the water. Lake Michigan is a deep blue this evening, almost violet. The lake is dotted with sailboats and powerboats; many, she assumes, are already anchored for the fireworks tonight. Behind them, people are streaming toward the grassy area overlooking the beach.

"Sometimes when I see Lake Michigan I think of Mike," she says. "I imagine him looking at the English Channel on the last day of his life."

She turns to Greg. "I used to get so *angry* knowing that he survived D-Day and then died the next day from stray sniper fire. Why? Why did he make it through that day only to die the next?"

Greg puts his arm around her shoulder. "I don't know, Red. I don't know. Some of the men I cared for in the field hospital would tell me that the man next to them was blown up, or in other cases, didn't have a scratch. It's a mystery who lived and who died. There was no rhyme or reason to it. Just chance."

"The last letter he sent Mom and Dad—he wrote it that morning," Vivian continues. "A few hours before he died. He said that he was fine, and he hoped the war would be over soon, so he could come home and marry Maggie."

"At least your parents had that letter," Greg says. "Sometimes—sometimes I didn't want to write my parents. I couldn't tell them what I was experiencing, and the cheerful letters I wrote to them sounded fake. But I knew if anything happened that would be all they would have, those letters."

"Dad would sit in the study, reading Mike's letters over and over again. Finally Mom put them away in a box in her closet." Vivian says.

Vivian is quiet for a moment thinking of her father in the study, reading glasses propped on his nose, holding a letter from Mike, and quickly folding the note and looking at her guiltily when she walked in the room, as if grief was something they were supposed to fold up in a box and hide. She focuses on counting the sailboats directly ahead—five, six, no, seven—and another colorful cluster of sails near the harbor.

Greg doesn't reply. Vivian wonders if he is thinking the same thing as she is, that if Mike had been standing two feet to the left or right, he would have come home, and Maggie and Mike would have married, and she and Greg might have married as well. She might have been a bride at twenty instead of an unmarried woman at fifty-one. They might have had children, cousins to Maggie and Mike's. So many what-ifs. So many possibilities were cut short.

"Penny for your thoughts?" Greg says.

"Thinking of the what-ifs."

"I like to think," Greg says slowly, "that Mike would have been happy for us. That we found each other again." He clears his throat. "But this afternoon you sounded like you're not sure." He turns and looks at her questioningly.

Vivian takes his hand and squeezes it.

"What if this doesn't work? That's what worries me. I've been so happy with you these past weeks, but what if it doesn't work between us? I'm not easy to be with, you know."

Greg turns to face her. "I'm not always either. If it doesn't work out, then it doesn't work out. We feel sad and then move on. But we tried. That's what counts."

Vivian's mouth feels dry. Her heart is pounding.

"Greg, I'm happy and terrified. So much could go wrong with us. Maybe our past should stay in the past."

"And so much could go right," he adds quietly. He turns and watches a gull wheeling above the water. "We won't know unless we try."

Vivian looks at the water in its many shades of blue. She loves walking by the lake every morning. Sometimes it's dark gray, sometimes deep blue, sometimes choppy, sometimes smooth. Sometimes she walks to the lake expecting it to be a smooth blue, and it's a turbulent gray. Other times she expects it to be a slate gray, and it's soothing blue. She never knows for sure until she sees it, and sometimes she's surprised because sometimes it's the opposite of what she expected, a vivid blue on a cloudy day.

Vivan takes a deep breath. "All right. Let's give this—not just the old college try, we'll give it—our best. I can do that. Try our best."

"We will," he says quietly. "We'll try, the very best try. And if it doesn't . . ."

He kisses her. "We may not have Paris, but we'll always have this." He gestures toward the lake.

Vivian laughs. "A view of Lake Michigan from Middleport on July 3, 1976."

The lake has darkened to a deep, glorious blue. Honey barks at a golden retriever trotting past and tugs at her leash.

"I think she's telling us she's ready to leave," Vivian laughs, and they head back to the house, hand in hand.

Chapter 35
Skylar
8:30 p.m.

Skye stands writing at the window looking at Lake Michigan, her journal spread out on the windowsill.

It's dusk, and the fireworks will start soon. The lake is deep blue now, maybe indigo blue, I guess. So much has happened today! I'll write more tomorrow about everything that happened with Grandma Kitty flying to Denver and Aunt Vivian showing up with her Greg, who I guess is her old boyfriend. Zack sort of kissed me, but it doesn't really count because he likes Jenny. I feel sad—she crosses it out and writes *disappointed, but it's okay. There are lots of other guys and, in any case, there are more important things to do than worry about some boy.*

It isn't exactly the truth. She does feel sad, not just disappointed, but maybe if she writes it, she will not be sad. Just a little disappointed. She thinks and writes again.

Dad talked to me. He doesn't really understand because he's old, but he said he liked a girl in junior high once who threw him over for some other guy, and then when he started dating Mom, he was happy that he could be with her. He said to be myself, but I am not sure who I am. I guess I'll figure it out. I hope so.

She sets down her pen and looks at the lake. It's almost dark now, and soon they will watch the fireworks, and then tomorrow will be July 4, 1976. The Bicentennial. A day she will always remember.

Chapter 36
Grace
8:35 p.m.

Grace lies on her bed, staring at the purple and pink stars painted on her ceiling. Mom stenciled the stars when Grace was five, and even though she's an adult now, Grace has never wanted to change them. Skye has stars on her ceiling, too. "Look at the stars and remember to reach for them," Mom told them when they were little.

Grace had gone to her room to change into shorts and a T-shirt and doesn't feel like going back outside just yet to converse with everyone.

She thinks about all that happened today. The party and talking with Aunt Vivian and her beau reappearing from the past. Grandma Kitty is flying to Denver for a trip through the national parks with her friend Agnes. Good for her, Grace thinks, even though she can't imagine Grandma Kitty hiking.

She thinks about the old couple dancing at the open house, coming close together, spinning apart, and coming together again. She is sure they were an old married couple, even though Aunt Vivian said they could have just met that day. No, they had a look of people who had known and loved each other for a long, long time.

She thinks about the conversation she and Ben had this morning, the same one they've had, repeatedly, all summer: stay in Wisconsin or go to France, and the question simmering beneath that—stay together or break up.

She stares at the delicate ring on her right ring finger. She slips it off, slides it back on, and studies the way the light sparkles off the tourmaline stone and the thin gold band.

Maybe they've been going at it the wrong way, round and round, each stuck in their own position, thinking that it's one or the other. Maybe there is another way.

Kitty and Agnes are poring over the maps spread out on the kitchen table. They are both tired, but too excited to go to bed just yet. Tomorrow they will attend the Fourth of July parade and enjoy the day with Scott, Jean, and their three boys. They will then spend a few days packing and buying supplies before they leave on Wednesday. Their plan is to drive down to the Grand Canyon and then circle back up to Zion, Bryce, Yellowstone, and Glacier National Park before returning to Colorado. They will alternate calls to their families. Agnes will call Scott on Mondays, Wednesdays, and Fridays, and Kitty will call Joe and Claire every Tuesday, Thursday, and Saturday, and they will both write postcards on Sunday evenings.

"We're having our adventure, Kitty," Agnes says as she marks a leg of their journey on the map with a yellow highlighter. "We're finally going on our trip to see the West that Miss Adams told us about in Girl Scouts."

Kitty pats Agnes's hand. Her friend's face is wrinkled, and her hair is sparse and gray, but the sparkle in her brown eyes is the same as it was sixty years ago.

"Yes, we are, my friend," Kitty replies. "We are."

Chapter 38
Grace
9:10 p.m.

They are all sitting inside the screened-in porch: her parents, Grandma Edna, Great-uncle Chester, Aunt Vivian, Greg, and Skye. Uncle Rob isn't here yet, but he called and told Dad that Sam came home a day early, and they'll be over soon. Her parents, Aunt Vivian, and Greg are each enjoying a gin and tonic. Grandma Edna has a glass of iced tea. Grace notices that she frowns whenever she takes a sip like she doesn't know what it is, or maybe, Grace thinks, she wishes it were a martini. Great-uncle Chester is having a brandy old-fashioned. Grace is drinking a Tab. The champagne at the reception made her drowsy, and she wants to stay up late tonight because she's getting together with Ben after the fireworks. She's nervous about what she's going to say to him.

She twists the ring around her finger. Again, she thinks about the old couple dancing together at the reception. She remembers the way they smiled at each other and laughed together.

The phone rings. Grace jumps up. "I'll get it!" she says. She scrambles past everyone and dashes into the kitchen and grabs the telephone receiver. "Hello?"

"Hey, Grace, it's me. We've got some food left over from the dinner rush and Mom packed some grilled chicken and meatballs for you guys. I'll bike over and drop it off. My dad said it was okay to take a break for a few minutes."

"We can pick it up tomorrow," Grace says. She hears the din of conversation and dishes clattering in the background, and she knows how busy the restaurant must be and that Ben will be missed.

"I'll come over," he says. "It's no problem." He pauses. "That is, if you want me to come over."

Grace swallows hard. "Okay, I'll meet you halfway. Meet me at the end of the street."

"Everything okay? You sound upset."

"No, I'm fine. Well, we'll talk. I'll see you there!" She hangs up the phone before he can say anything more.

She doesn't know why, but she suddenly needs to see him alone, now. She can't wait until later tonight to talk to him. She needs to talk to him now, at night, under the stars; it is outside, in private, that she can say to him what she needs and wants to say.

"I'm meeting Ben, be right back," she says as she hurries through the porch before Mom can ask her any questions.

She half runs, half walks, to the end of Lakeview Street. The street is crammed with people headed to the bluff overlooking the lake to watch the fireworks, and the grassy expanse is filled with families unfolding lawn chairs and spreading blankets on the ground. Kids run up and down the street waving sparklers. Couples walk arm and arm.

She stands at the corner of Lakeview and Elm Streets ignoring the river of people flowing around her, looking for Ben. She spots him, pushing his Schwinn 10-speed through the crowd with one hand and carrying an overstuffed backpack in the other. He draws closer, and she sees that his sandy hair is tousled, there's a sheen of sweat across his face, and his McLaren's Pub & Grill T-shirt is wrinkled and stained.

He kisses her, looks at her questioningly, and then says, "Mom says to put this in the fridge right away. C'mon. I'll walk back to the house with you."

"Ben," she kisses him back. "Let's walk for a few minutes before going back, okay?

"But the chicken—"

She presses her finger against his lip. "Don't worry about the darn chicken right now. Please, let's just talk for a moment."

He looks at her, puzzled, and nods. "Okay."

She leads him to a side street that is quieter. She turns to Ben and slips off her ring.

"Sell it," she says. "Please. Take it."

Ben looks at her, then at the ring in her palm, and then back at her. He looks heartbroken. He swallows, shakes his head *no* and gently covers her hand with his own.

"I knew this was going to happen." His voice is husky. "I understand. You need to go. You can't be tied down. But the ring is a gift to you. It's yours to keep, do what you want with it."

"Ben," Grace kisses Ben again, this time harder. "I'm *not* breaking up with you. I want *you*—and I want you to sell back the ring and use it for a plane ticket. To France."

"What do you mean?" He looks half hopeful, half anxious.

"Come to France in December." She's nervous but plunges on. "After you finish your last exam, get on a plane and come over to France. Let's celebrate Christmas together. We can go the Christmas markets and maybe take the train to Italy."

He is quiet, studying her face in the twilight.

"You're serious?"

She nods and smiles. "I am!"

"We spend a month together in France. And then?"

Grace laughs. "I don't know! Maybe we will come back to Wisconsin together. The program lasts a year but, like you said, maybe I can just go for a semester.

I mean, what are they going to do? Kick me out of school for coming back early? I'll come home and spend the second semester in Madison. Or—"

"But it's a full-year program."

She shrugs. "I guess I realized today that nothing is set in stone. We're young. We can make our own rules, right? It's 1976, not 1956, and I can come back anytime I want."

"Or I stay with you?" he says.

She shakes her head. "Maybe. No, you're going to veterinary school. You've got a schedule to keep with your classes. You can't afford to miss a semester of school."

He smiles. "Or can I? We'll figure it out, one way or another."

"Our parents are going to freak out if we're not there for Christmas, but we have years to spend with them."

Ben puts his arm around her, and they look at Lake Michigan. It's the in-between time when it's no longer day and not yet night. The fireworks will start soon, but for a moment, the crowds and noise seem far away, and it's just the two of them, gazing at the lake on a beautiful summer evening as the stars begin to appear in the sky.

And an in-between time for them as well, she thinks, not quite together, and not quite apart. She doesn't know what will happen. But she understands now that sometimes when two people are going around and around, the best way to stop going around in circles is to leap right through.

The fireworks explode and sizzle. Red, blue, green, and purple bursts of light, like bits of colored glass. The scent of sulfur drifts through the air. The crowd *ooh*s and *ah*s and claps after each burst of lights. And it's only the first night. There will be an even bigger fireworks display tomorrow.

The family has moved from the porch to the driveway to watch the show. Edna and Chester sit in lawn chairs near the porch door. Joe, Claire, Rob, and Sam stand by them. Skye sits on a bench next to the porch, petting Honey, who barks and whines at each pop of fireworks. Vivian and Greg are sitting on the hood of Vivian's Mustang. Grace and Ben stand at the end of the driveway, arms around each other.

"I'm sorry, sweetheart, about what I said earlier," Joe whispers to Claire. "Tomorrow let's talk about your coffee shop idea."

Claire nods and squeezes his hand.

"Mom and Dad?" They turn to see Grace and Ben, who have walked back up the driveway to stand by them. They are holding hands and smiling; whatever tension there was between them this morning is gone.

"We have something to tell you," Grace says.

"We're—I mean Grace and I—" Ben says. "We're going to spend Christmas together in France."

"I see," says Claire. This was certainly a new development.

"Between semesters," Grace adds.

"That's good news," Joe says heartily. He turns to Claire and raises his eyebrows. It's his *let's talk about this later* look.

Grace smiles. "It will all work out, Mom and Dad! Really."

"I better get back to work," Ben says. "Enjoy the fireworks, Mr. and Mrs. Ames."

Grace takes Ben's hand and the two head back down the driveway.

Joe puts his arm around Claire. "I'll miss our girl at Christmas."

"Thank God she isn't pregnant," Claire says.

"They'll come back either married or not speaking," she adds. She kisses her husband's cheek. "But I'm not going to worry about that tonight."

As Skye pets Honey, who nuzzles her shoulder, she absently wonders what her parents were talking about with Grace and Ben, but her mind is on the day that is now ending and what happened at the concert. She didn't get kissed, or, well, she sort of got kissed, but it wasn't what she thought it would be like. Zack is her friend, or maybe he's not really a friend. She's not sure. She wants to be kissed again, someday, but by a boy who really likes her and when it feels right. There's no rush; after all, she just turned thirteen eleven days ago.

She watches the fireworks burst, shimmer, and fall. She then looks around at her family. Grandma Edna seems confused, but happy, tugging at Great-uncle Chester's shirtsleeve like a little kid and pointing at the fireworks. Chester pats her arm and chews on the end of his cigar. Mom and Dad are standing by them, looking happy like they've made up from their fight this afternoon, something about a store downtown that she overheard. Grace and Ben are at the end of the driveway. They kiss, and Ben hops on his bike and waves goodbye. Aunt Vivian and Greg are sitting on the hood of her Mustang, and Skye thinks it's neat that old people still want to act like teenagers. Uncle Rob and Sam showed up later, around nine. She's glad for Uncle Rob that Sam came home a few days early because Aunt Amy has been gone all summer, and she heard Dad tell Mom that he thought Uncle Rob and Aunt Amy were going to get a divorce. She feels bad for Uncle Rob, and Aunt Amy, who Skye thinks always looks a little sad. She hopes Aunt Amy is happier up north.

Fireworks burst into the air again, pink and blue that remind Skye of the colors of the strings of beads that Grandma Kitty likes to wear that match her dresses. She wonders if Grandma Kitty and her friend Agnes are watching fireworks right now. Even though Grandma Kitty is in Colorado, she told Skye she would be here in spirit. Everyone's here. All of them. Her family. The people she loves.

When she is eighty years old, she will remember this moment. She will remember the day, this Bicentennial Fourth of July weekend.

Epilogue
July 4, 2001 & July 3, 2026

"What did you do to celebrate the twenty-fifth anniversary of HerArt?" Vivian asks. It's beautiful weather for Independence Day, and Claire, Joe, and Vivian are sitting in the backyard in the early evening, enjoying the lake breeze before the mosquitoes drive them inside. Further out on the lawn, Grace, Ben, Skye, and her boyfriend Max are wrapping up a game of croquet.

"We had an open house with women in the community contributing photos and paintings of what freedom means to them. Lots of interesting ways to look at freedom! Everything from letting your hair go gray to buying your own home. And Alma gave a talk about her book on the stories of Black women business owners in Middleport in the 1800s. The *Middleport Gazette* published a nice story about the reception, too."

"It sounds like it was lovely," Vivian says "I'm sorry I wasn't there. But I look forward to stopping by tomorrow."

"We missed you, but I'm glad you had a good trip."

Vivian returned two days ago from a Rhine River cruise. She needed to get away, she told Claire, after Greg's death in March.

"Rob and Beth said they might go on a cruise next year to Alaska," Joe chimes in the conversation. After Rob and Amy divorced, Rob dated Lisa for a while, whom everyone liked, but Rob wasn't ready to plunge into another relationship so soon, and they'd broken up after a year, and a few years later she'd quit teaching after her mother died and moved to North Carolina to escape the cold winters. Eventually Rob met Beth and they married five years ago. Today they are visiting Sam and his family in Green Bay.

Joe stands up. "We'll be moving inside soon, so I'll bring the cooler to the porch."

"Here, let me help you!" Claire says. Ever since Joe had a heart attack while shoveling snow last January—thank goodness it was a mild one—she worries about him overexerting himself, even though the doctor has said he could resume normal activities.

"I'm fine," he says firmly. It has been a struggle to get Joe to slow down. He reaches down and starts dragging the cooler toward the porch. Max drops his croquet mallet and jogs over to Joe.

"How about if we do it together?" Max says.

Joe grunts and nods. Max grabs the handle and drags the cooler toward the door with Joe nudging the cooler from the back.

Claire likes Skye's friend, date, boyfriend, whatever the right term is now. He seems to be more than a date, but not yet a full-fledged—what is it, *significant other*—that's the term Skye uses. Claire prefers the word beau, an old-fashioned term, perhaps, but one that sounds more romantic. Max reminds her, in a way, with his gentleness and steadfastness, of Uncle Chester, who died seven years ago at age ninety-seven.

"Max is nice," Claire murmurs to Vivian. "Joe and I like him."

"Skye finally realized that a relationship doesn't need to be an endless game of chess," Vivian comments. "When she asked for my advice—and I only gave advice when she asked—I told her she should never compromise on character, but could consider compromising on things that, in the end, don't really matter, like, oh, hating opera. I told her she can go to the opera with her friends; what matters is a loving man will be waiting for her when she gets home."

"I simply want Skye to be happy," Claire says. Then she adds, to change the subject, as Max and Joe return, "Do you remember the Bicentennial weekend?"

"What? Oh, I see," Vivian nods toward Max. "Yes, I do. I brought Greg, and I think you nearly fell over with surprise to see me with him again."

Claire smiles at the memory. She was annoyed with Vivian that Bicentennial weekend, but she was happy that Vivian and Greg found each other again, and that she and Vivian have grown closer over the past years.

"That was the year that Mom went on her first trip with Agnes, too."

"I remember that! Your dash to the airport to say good-bye. How many trips did they go on before Agnes broke her hip and they couldn't travel anymore?"

Claire counts on her fingers. "Let's see, the national parks trip was the first one. Then the train trip to Gettysburg, Washington, D.C., the drive through New England, Disney World, New York, London and Paris, and Hawaii."

"Your Mom and Agnes packed in a lot of travel in seven years," Joe comments as he sits down. He turns to Max. "My mother-in-law and her friend got the travel bug when they were in their seventies and traveled all over."

Max grins. "Sounds like my grandmother. She took her last trip, a cruise, when she was eighty-five."

"I'm two years older than Mom was back then," Vivian says thoughtfully. "Hard to believe. I don't feel seventy-six."

Vivian does not look seventy-six either, Claire reflects. Her sister's hair is dyed red, and she suspects she's had some work done on her face, which is remarkably smooth for her age, and she still has her straight posture and brisk walk.

Claire decided to go the natural route with her aging, letting her blond hair fade into gray and trying, as Betty says, to "embrace her wrinkles," although she uses sunscreen and moisturizer.

"People seemed older, then," Claire remarks. "They looked older, too, or maybe more formal. I always think of Mom in her pastel dresses, string of pearls, and clip-on earrings."

"But my favorite picture of her is the one from their trip to Yellowstone," Claire adds. "Her and Agnes in their jeans and checkered shirts and hiking sticks."

"Your mom sounds like she was an interesting lady," Max says. Skye wanders over and touches Max's shoulder.

"Who, my grandma? Oh, she was great. I loved visiting her."

"A side of Mom we had no idea existed," Vivian remarks. "Mom the Girl Scout and adventurer."

"It doesn't seem like twenty-five years since the Bicentennial," Claire remarks. "If I hadn't gone to Dillworth's to buy paper cups and napkins, HerArt might have never come into existence."

"And if I hadn't invited Greg to come with me that day, I might have ended our connection," Vivian says. "You know, I think it was bringing him here that made me brave enough to move forward. I miss him so," Vivian adds wistfully. "But I am grateful for the twenty-five years we had together."

Twenty-five years since the Bicentennial. How quickly time had gone. Grace, the same age as Claire was in 1976, and Skye nearly forty, though in her shorts and T-shirt and her hair pulled back in a ponytail she looks barely older than the girl she was a quarter century earlier.

Claire thinks back to how busy she used to be—there was always so much to do! She was always in motion, taking the girls to lessons and sports, and after they grew older, helping Mom and running HerArt. Now time has slowed down. She is selling HerArt to Gil Romero's daughter, who she hired as a part-time assistant ten years ago and who now manages the store. After Joe's heart attack, she realized that she wants to slow down and savor time with their daughters and grandchildren.

And if she's lucky, she might see America's 250th birthday. She can't imagine what might happen in the next twenty-five years in the country—good things she hopes—but if her family is with her, they can weather anything.

"And that's a game! "Ben says. "Congrats, Skye and Max, you beat us by a point."

"Good game, guys," Max says. He shakes Ben's hand.

Grace likes Skye's friend. For twenty years, Skye had a string of what Grace considered to be stuffy, fussy academic types—not that there's anything wrong with that; after all, Skye is a professor—but it seemed like Skye approached dating like she was writing a research paper, all analysis and introspection. Maybe that cerebral distance is what Skye really wants, but Grace thinks Skye needs someone to love her like Ben loves her, wholeheartedly and loyally, and Max seems like he might be that guy.

"What's new with the kids?" Skye asks.

Grace and Ben had called their twins, Ethan and Amelia, who are counselors at two different summer camps in northern Wisconsin, just before they had started their game of croquet.

"They're fine. Enjoying being camp counselors and not missing their parents," Grace says, smiling.

"I'm sure they do," Skye says, "but they're fifteen. They're not going to admit it." She leans over to pull a wicket out of the grass.

"You look lost in thought," Ben whispers to Grace as he packs the mallets in the canvas bag.

"I'm thinking of the Bicentennial Fourth when we decided to go to France."

Ben grins and kisses her. "You mean you decided we were going to France, and I loved every minute of it, my dear."

They had spent a glorious month traveling through Europe. On Christmas Eve they had gone up to Strasbourg, wandered through a Christmas market, slipped into a church and attended a Christmas service, and then called their parents, inserting every franc they had into the pay phone so they could wish their families a Merry Christmas. Grace had decided to forgo the second semester of her year abroad after all. They had come home together in late January, finished their last year and a half of school, firmly a couple. It was three years later that they broke up, temporarily. Ben was attending the University of Minnesota Veterinary School, and she had followed him up to Minneapolis. Ben had wanted to get married right away, but she had said no, they should wait until he graduated. They lived together, which Mom and Dad hated, and then she was grumpy because he was immersed in classes and labs, and she didn't like teaching French. They had a blow-up, and, just like Aunt Vivian had done in 1945, she'd gone off to Chicago, where she worked a couple of office jobs and sort of fell into the IT field because she was the only one in the office willing to figure out what was wrong with the desktop computer, and now to her amazement—she was an un-techy comparative literature major with a French minor, for goodness' sakes—she is an information technology consultant for veterinary practices.

Three years after they broke up, she'd been home visiting Mom and Dad for the Fourth, moping that the busy lawyer she had sort of been seeing had dumped her. She bumped into Ben at Dillworth's, of all places, and he told her things had ended with the veterinary student he'd been dating. A nice person, but he realized he didn't love her. They'd watched the fireworks together that night, and, well, that was that. All their love for each other came rushing back. She moved back to Middleport; they married a year later.

Grace is glad they can spend the Fourth with her parents. She's worried about Dad, even though he's doing well with his cardiac rehab. She's happy to be here for Aunt Vivian, too.

She takes her husband's hand.

"Happy Fourth, Ben," she says.

He kisses her. "Happy Fourth, and many, many
more."

Skye watches as Max lifts the end of the cooler and helps Dad lug it inside. One of the many things she loves about Max is his kindness. He's happy with his life, content with who he is as a tax accountant in his own small practice, and she's noticed that his happiness radiates outward by the way he treats others with thoughtfulness and kindness. They've been together a year now, and she suspects at some point he may pop the question. The thought makes her both excited and nervous.

This relationship with Max was a surprise. Her married friend Michelle had suggested meeting her accountant. "He's adorable, Skye!" Although *accountant* and *adorable* sounded like an oxymoron, Max was sweet and cheerful and, yes, adorable, with his dimples and deep blue eyes. His ex-wife had left him for a woman three years earlier. He had shrugged when he told her, "Yes, it hurt at first, but I'm glad she's happy."

She had always thought of relationships as a challenge, a puzzle to be solved, with intriguing, intellectual, interesting men. She supposed it was an extreme reaction to first dating Billy in high school. After two months they agreed they were better off as friends, and they are still good friends, in fact, and he's married now to a lawyer who's just as neurotic as him, and they took over his dad's practice, and then Zack, whom she dated the summer after junior year in high school against her better judgment (teenaged hormones!), until his ambivalence and flirtatiousness with other girls broke her heart. After high school, Zack moved to Austin, and she's heard through the grapevine that he's a fairly successful musician and a part-time bartender living with a woman who is in his band, and Skye is happy for him. Starting in college, she had embarked on relationships with one cerebral, complicated man after another. She's worked with a therapist for two years now, and she's figured out that relationships don't have to be like either a headlong dive with an exciting but unsuitable man, or a slog through mud with an emotionally unavailable one. Then just when she had sworn to Aunt Vivian that she was going to be single forever, she had met Max, and she had discovered a new way to love and be loved.

She thinks back to the Bicentennial weekend, which she remembers vividly, not only because she wrote about it in her journal, but because it felt like something had changed that day. She was almost kissed and had moved from a girl to a teenager.

She will write about this Fourth in her journal later, too. She keeps one, even though she's not sure why. Maybe she'll re-read her teenaged journals one day and write a memoir about growing up in the 1970s. Or maybe she'll write about how America celebrated its 200th birthday, at least in her small town in Wisconsin. It's an idea she has, something that she's scribbling in a notebook between grading papers and planning lectures.

She remembers that day twenty-five years ago, and she will remember this day too. Not because anything remarkable has happened, but because it's been an ordinary, good day, and just like she tells her students when they are studying *Our Town*, it's the happy, ordinary days that are the ones to remember.

"It's been a great day," she says to Max.

"It has indeed."

He takes her hand. "Should we join the others?"

As they walk toward the porch, she turns and glances at the yard, at the fireflies bobbing in the twilight, the puffy clouds tinged with pink, the empty velvety green lawn where they had just played croquet. Then she looks ahead toward the porch, toward her family, waiting for her and Max, and she thinks:

Remember this Fourth of July.

Remember this moment.

Remember this day.

Claire sits between her daughters on the bench overlooking Lake Michigan. The wood and metal bench with the graceful, curved armrests is on a strip of grass across the street from her old house, now owned by Grace and Ben, with whom she has lived for the past ten years. The back of the bench has a bronze plaque with the inscription, *In memory of Joe Ames, who loved the view of the lake*. Claire and her daughters pooled their money and purchased a bench from the city in honor of their husband and father.

It's a beautiful evening. The sky is deepening from blue to indigo, the clouds are tinged with pink, and the lake is smooth. A few sailboats still dot the lake, as sailors squeeze in a last few minutes of sailing before the sun sets.

Skye drove from Madison to visit her for a few days; early tomorrow morning she will drive back to spend the holiday with Max and their daughter Vivian, named after her great-aunt. Skye's been coming to visit more often. Each time she leaves she looks at Claire with an anxious expression, as though she's worried she'll never see her mother again, which could very well be true.

This is, Claire suspects, her last Fourth of July. She's ninety-four years old and she can feel in her bones that her body is failing her. She gets dizzy and short of breath but has told her doctor firmly that she does not want any more tests, thank you very much. She doesn't mind dying soon, if that's what is to be. She's looking forward to being reunited with Joe. She had a dream a few nights ago in which she saw Joe sitting in a lawn chair in the backyard of the apartment he rented in college. He looked young again, like he was twenty-five, and he smiled and blew her a kiss.

"You okay, Mom?" Grace pats her hand. Grace is sixty-nine now, and as she ages, she reminds Claire more and more of her own mother, Kitty, petite and plump now with the same beautiful skin that her mother had.

"Let's get in before mosquitoes come out," Skye says. Even in her sixties, she still has that coltish look with her long legs and her hair, which is now silvery gray and as unruly as ever.

"In a minute," Claire murmurs. If this is to be her last Fourth of July eve, she wants to enjoy it a little longer.

Claire closes her eyes. She remembers that day, July 3, 1976, when she and Alma and Betty had laughed and toasted one another, her chance encounter with Gil Romero that ended up changing her life, the mad dash to the airport, and Vivian's surprise appearance with Greg.

"Penny for your thoughts, Mom," Skye says.

Claire opens her eyes. "Oh, thinking of July Fourths from the past. Spending the holiday with your father when he was in college. The parties years ago with your Illinois cousins. The Bicentennial when we celebrated on our own."

"Remember the day," Skye says. "That's what I wrote in my journal in 1976. I wanted to remember every moment. It felt like such a special day. Celebrating two hundred years! But—"

"But what?" Grace asks.

"Maybe there's a part that I forgot to write down," Skye says. She closes her eyes, inhales the sweet evening air, opens her eyes, and looks at the lake in its twilight beauty.

"Remember the day, oh, yes—but first, live the day."

"Live the day," Grace echoes.

Claire smiles and nods.

Author's Note

I have vivid memories of the Bicentennial—the Bicentennial quarters, ornaments, and knickknacks; the fire hydrants in town painted red, white, and blue; the Bicentennial Minutes television spots that provided bite-sized lessons in American history; the local high school that performed the musical *1776*; the scenes on television of the tall ships gliding through New York Harbor; and the goofy fun of a country shaking off years of discord and discontent to celebrate its anniversary. The local Fourth of July parade that year was especially big and festive, and my parents threw a Bicentennial bash for family and friends. My mother dressed up as Betsy Ross and my aunt as Uncle Sam.

Yet memories are imperfect and incomplete, and the internet was an invaluable resource for checking random facts such as 1970s car models and the Brewers schedule on July 3, 1976. Newspapers.com provided access to papers from July 1976, and reading the faded pages of a diary and looking at family snapshots sparked inspiration and smiles.

As I write this note just months ahead of publication, we are about to celebrate America's 250th birthday. Unchanged are the families who will come together gathering for fireworks displays, parades will line the main streets, and the store aisles will be full of commemorative products.

Family has always been a core source of love and support. This story was inspired by my extended family—my grandmother, aunts, uncles, and cousins—who showed up faithfully at 7 a.m. every year, rain or shine, to sit at the same corner on Main Street to watch the Fourth of July parade with my parents, sister, and me before we gathered at my parents' house for food, laughter, and fun. This story is fictional and the town, characters, scenes, and events come from my imagination. The spirit of the story, however, of an ordinary family dreaming of possibilities for the future, figuring out love, and adjusting to changing times were inspired by my own memories of growing up in the 1970s, as well as the stories my mother and grandmother told to knit our family history.

Acknowledgements

The transformation of a vague idea of a story set during the American Bicentennial into a completed novella was made possible only with the support, encouragement, and guidance of many people, to whom I am deeply thankful.

The three fabulous women of Fresh Water Press—Tara Huck, Tracey Koach, and Peggy Turnbull—had a vision of a boutique press focused on writers who have a connection to Wisconsin's lakeshore, and they made their vision a reality. A huge thank you to the Fresh Water Press, especially editor Tara Huck for her astute editing, warmth, good humor, patience, and belief in my novella; Tracey Koach for her guidance with the legal and contractual aspects of publishing; Peggy Turnbull for her eagle-eyed editing; and engagement manager Sophia Dramm for marketing and social media assistance. Vagabond Creative Studio designed the marvelous cover that perfectly captures that 1970s vibe.

Writing circle colleagues Billie Braeger and Karin Derenne created a warm environment to share work and gave spot-on feedback. The Wisconsin Writers Association is a rich source of writing resources and fellowship; I wish I had joined it years ago! Fellow WWA member Victoria Lynn Smith became a pen-pal friend, and her insights on writing and publishing were so helpful.

At Girl Scout camp, we would cheerfully sing, "Make new friends and keep the old," a sentiment close to my heart, and my friends have always encouraged my writing, read my work, and, most of all, have been dear and treasured friends.

A big hug to my sister Pam and brother-in-law Pat, who are always there for me. And many hugs to my niece Britt, and my nephew Shane, and their beautiful families. Being an aunt and a great-aunt is the greatest joy in my life.

I wish my parents, who passed along their own love of reading, were here to see the launch of this book. Mom took me to the library and patiently waited while I chose an armful of books. Dad would return from a business trip with a new Nancy Drew book tucked in his briefcase, and in later years he built sturdy oak shelves for me to fill with books.

My kind and steadfast other half, Peter, is a brilliant writer who had a sterling forty-plus-year career as a sportswriter; his love and support mean the world to me.

Finally, this book is dedicated to anyone who happily wanders through a bookstore and gets lost in a good book, as well as to anyone who sits down at their laptop or flips open a notebook and, in this time of cold algorithms and fractured attention spans, takes a leap of faith, and begins to write a story.

Julie A. Jacob is a communications professional and freelance writer. She has an MFA in creative writing from Roosevelt University, and her creative nonfiction works and essays have been published in *Midwest Prairie Review, On Wisconsin, Open, Under the Sun,* and several editions of the Tall Grass Writers Guild annual anthology. Some of her work is featured in a self-published collection of essays, *Two States of Single: Essays on Love, Family, and Living Solo,* available on Kindle. This is her first novel. She lives in southeastern Wisconsin with her poodle and enjoys spending time with family and friends.

The Fresh Water Press was founded February 2024 in Two Rivers, Wisconsin, and specializes in books by writers who live in or write about the northeastern Wisconsin lakeshore. The Press publishes in several genres and welcomes submissions from underrepresented authors and unique voices.

Titles from Fresh Water Press:

Opening Nights: A Collection of Theater Stories

Ghost(ed) Woman & the Electric Purple Pants
  by Emilie Lindemann

Dial Down: Holistic Strategies to Move from Chaos to Calm
  by Raquel Durden

RADIO STARR
  by Lisa Lehmann

Bicentennial Eve: A Wisconsin Novella
  by Julie A. Jacob

www.ingramcontent.com/pod-product-compliance
Lightning Source LLC
Chambersburg PA
CBHW051956150726

47999CB00004B/1408